MASTERS
—— AND ——
SERVANTS

BOOKS BY PIERRE MICHON IN ENGLISH

Small Lives (*Vies minuscules,* 1984)
Rimbaud the Son (*Rimbaud le fils,* 1991)
The Origin of the World (*La Grande Beune,* 1996)
Winter Mythologies and Abbots (*Mythologies d'hiver,* 1997; *Abbés,* 2002)
The Eleven (*Les Onze,* 2009)

MASTERS
—— AND ——
SERVANTS

by
Pierre Michon

Translated, Illustrated, and with a
New Introduction by Wyatt Mason

Yale
UNIVERSITY PRESS
New Haven and London

A MARGELLOS
WORLD REPUBLIC OF LETTERS BOOK

The Margellos World Republic of Letters is dedicated to making literary works from around the globe available in English through translation. It brings to the English-speaking world the work of leading poets, novelists, essayists, philosophers, and playwrights from Europe, Latin America, Africa, Asia, and the Middle East to stimulate international discourse and creative exchange.

First Yale University Press edition 2013.
First English edition published by Mercury House in 1997.
Originally published as *Vie de Joseph Roulin, Maîtres et serviteurs,* and *Le Roi du bois.* Copyright © Éditions Verdier, 1988, 1990, and 1996, respectively.
Introduction copyright © 2013 by Wyatt Mason.
Translation and illustrations copyright © 1997 by Wyatt Mason.

All rights reserved.
This book may not be reproduced, in whole or in part, including illustrations, in any form (beyond that copying permitted by Sections 107 and 108 of the U.S. Copyright Law and except by reviewers for the public press), without written permission from the publishers.

Yale University Press books may be purchased in quantity for educational, business, or promotional use. For information, please e-mail sales.press@yale.edu (U.S. office) or sales@yaleup.co.uk (U.K. office).

Designed and typeset by Thomas Christensen and Kirsten Janene-Nelson.

Printed in the United States of America.

Library of Congress Control Number: 2013940418
ISBN: 978-0-300-18069-5 (pbk.)

A catalogue record for this book is available from the British Library.

10 9 8 7 6 5 4 3 2 1

Table of Contents

Introduction by Wyatt Mason   ix

MASTERS AND SERVANTS

The Life of Joseph Roulin   3

God Is Never Through   53

"... Io mi voglio divertir"   87

Trust This Sign   119

The King of the Wood   159

Notes   177

Introduction
WYATT MASON

In July 1995, when I was living in a small town in southern New Mexico, I received a letter in my post office box from Guy Davenport. Davenport was sixty-eight; I was twenty-six. He was the most learned literary person I'd ever heard of: author of forty books, MacArthur fellow, poet, fiction writer, critic, the first man to write a doctoral dissertation on James Joyce at Oxford University. I was eking out a living by substitute teaching French at a high school in the sixth-poorest county in America, a school where the majority of my students spoke Spanish as their first language. Ten days beforehand, I had sent Davenport a letter; with it, I included the manuscript of a little book. I came to the little book by chance while studying in Paris in the winter of 1990. For an independent study in translation I was undertaking, I was told to pick an author who hadn't been translated into English. A twenty-year-old who had no sense of contemporary French writing, I solicited suggestions from my professors. To a one, they came back with the same name: Pierre Michon. They described him as not merely the finest contemporary French writer yet to make his way into English, but the finest living French writer—a fervently held minority opinion, then as now, but not, as I would come to understand, an indefensible one. Of his five books, the criterion by which I selected the little novella I would translate, "Vie de Joseph Roulin," was, I concede, sophisticated: I picked the shortest one. As it would turn out, it was also arguably the best of them, a story that—following the eighteen months it took me to translate the little novel's sixty-three pages—I would love enough to spend the next eight years finding an American publisher for it.

I'd completed the translation in June 1991, but it turned out that my not knowing a soul in the world of letters made it somewhat difficult to advance the cause of a dense novella by an obscure Frenchman. I wrote to publishing houses, unbidden. Responses came, but creepingly. Through the years, a folder slowly fattened with rejections. When verdicts arrived, many were surprisingly frank ("It's kind of weird") and others frankly surprising ("This guy doesn't know how to write"). Nearly five years in, I had yet to receive one jot of encouraging news as a result of my mailings. Even so, I remained peculiarly sure that what I had in my hands was worth sharing.

One afternoon, after a particularly memorable morning of substitute teaching—I had ridden my bicycle the five miles to work and had been caught in a desert thunderstorm that left me dripping wet upon arrival, puddles forming under my feet as I attempted to teach the subjunctive to my nineteen-year-old tenth graders—I returned home where, still moist and not in the cheeriest of moods, my eyes hit upon the spine of Davenport's *The Geography of the Imagination:* essays on writing that had often been dismissed as weird, at first—the work of that James Joyce fellow, for one; and that of Kenneth Gangemi, Louis Zukovsky, Charles Olson, Paul Metcalf, and many more. It occurred to me that I should send the Michon along to Davenport. If he didn't like it, my translation wasn't any good.

What did Davenport find inside that envelope I sent him? For one thing, my cover letter: blessedly short but mercilessly overwritten. I was writing to a great man, a novel activity for me, and had attempted a great epistolary style, an adoption that by all rights should have been impeded by whatever agency oversees the elimination of the sorts of sentences that muscle, flex, groan, and grouse their way into the reader's treasure box of bon mots by overworking the language—sentences such as this one. ("I have to hold very tightly to the edges of your letters," Davenport would write to me in later months when we had begun to correspond on other matters. "Simplicity," he advised, "offends no one, clarity delights all.")

Davenport's reply to my overwritten plea was clear. "I've only read twenty pages of 'The Life of Joseph Roulin,'" read his typewritten response, a letter which I read in something close to shock as I crossed the railroad tracks that bordered the post office, heading down the dirt road that led to my house, "but it is already sufficiently compelling that you should send it on my recommendation to the following publishers." Davenport named his publisher in New York; another in San Francisco; a third in Boston. "It used to be unscrupulous to send a manuscript to more than one publisher at a time, but now it's standard procedure. Anyway, publishers don't have a scruple to their name."

TWO YEARS LATER, one of the three publishers Davenport recommended to me, Mercury House, a small, now defunct press in San Francisco, issued a first edition of the book you have in your hands, a book that included and includes that novella sent to Davenport by a stranger, "The Life of Joseph Roulin."

The proper name in the story's title may be familiar to you: Joseph Roulin was a postman in Arles, France, toward the end of the nineteenth century, and he and his wife and children were painted and drawn a number of times by a transplant to their town, Vincent van Gogh. These paintings now hang in museums around the world, and stories about their creation may be found in a few of the letters that van Gogh wrote to his brother, Theo, in which he mentions Roulin and his family. Beyond these paintings and those letters, there is little information about the moments the Roulins shared with the man now famous for being, as Michon puts it, "the patron saint of the beaux arts."

In part, Michon's novella can be seen as an enactment of Henry James's conception of the artistic struggle that appears in "The Middle Years," his short story about a novelist: "We work in the dark—we do what we can—we give what we have. Our doubt is our passion, and our passion is our task. The rest is the madness of art." As Davenport writes in an afterword to a collection of his own fiction,

Twelve Stories, "Making things is so human that psychology and philosophy have gotten nowhere in trying to account for it." Fiction, he felt, was a place for such explorations. Many of Davenport's own stories seek the force—invisible, ineffable—that might have animated a particular maker. *Tatlin!*, Davenport's first collection, features stories in which Edgar Allan Poe, Franz Kafka, and Vladimir Tatlin all figure. As such, and in retrospect, it's easy to imagine the kinship that Davenport as an artist would have felt for Michon and his own, not dissimilar explorations. Like Davenport, Michon manages to evade one clear potential pitfall of stories about famous artists: the reductive reflex that would try to explain the source of a particular masterpiece, to "solve" the question of where it came from. This is emphatically not what Michon's and Davenport's stories seek to dramatize. Rather, both men's tales find ways of plausibly conjuring the human connections in an artist's world that might have kept him alive while working in the dark. These are stories ultimately about friendship: what we give to those who make the pain to which we all are subject just another habit of being.

Pain and friendship are at the center of "The Life of Joseph Roulin," as well as at the hearts of the four novellas that join it here. All of them revolve around names we know because of the images they left: Goya, in "God Is Never Through"; Watteau, in " . . . Io mi voglio divertir"; Lorentino, an obscure disciple of Piero della Francesca, in "Trust This Sign"; and an unnamed follower of Claude Lorraine, in "The King of the Wood." The painters here could be dancers or singers or writers: what's universal in the artistic urge is the compulsion to offer the world a masterpiece that could compete with it, and the way that compulsion can wear away at the very spirit that gives it life.

As the arranger of the words of these stories already perfectly arranged in French, I have a stake in making claims about the fineness of what follows here, but it's a borrowed wealth. On the day he wrote me now nearly twenty years ago, Davenport acted as a friend, not yet to me, but to Michon.

MASTERS AND SERVANTS

> For as they were unable to distinguish between that of J.C. and those of the thieves, they placed them in the middle of the town, awaiting God's glory to manifest.
>
> —J. DA VARAGINE, *Legenda aurea*

The Life of Joseph Roulin

for Jacqueline

> *Marthe:* Is everything worth its price?
> *Thomas Pollock Nageoire:* Never.
>
> PAUL CLAUDEL, *The Exchange*

ONE OF THEM HAD BEEN stationed there by the Post Office, arbitrarily or perhaps according to his own wishes; the other had gone there because of the books he had read; because it was The South, where he believed that money might go further, that women were more favorable, and that the skies were excessive, Japanese. Because he was running away. Chance dropped them into Arles, in 1888. Different as they were, they enjoyed each other's company; in any case, the appearance of the one, the elder, pleased the other enough that he painted him four or five times: so we believe we know what he looked like that year, at forty-seven, the way we know how Louis XIV looked throughout his life, or how Innocent X looked in 1650; and in his portraits, he wears his hat as a king wears his crown, he's seated like a Pope, that's enough. We also know a few trifles about his life that he would be surprised to see, beneath his very face, in the verbose footnotes of all-knowing books. We know, for example, that at the end of 1888, the Post Office transferred him from Arles to Marseille; whether a promotion due to his zeal or a demotion due to his hangovers, we don't know; we're certain that he saw Vincent for the last time at the Arles hospital in February of the following year—this Vincent who was well on his way to being transferred from the bedlam of Arles to the bedlam in Saint-Rémy, before the big transfer to Auvers that in July of '90 did him in. We don't know what they said to each other at the very end. In what little van Gogh wrote about him, it's clear that Roulin was alcoholic and republican—which is to say that his words and beliefs were republican, and he was, in fact, an alcoholic—with an atheistic deportment that the absinthe encouraged; he was a big talker, voluble and occasionally profane, but a good guy, and his fraternal behavior toward the suffering painter made this clear. He wore a great beard, shaped like an axe, rich to paint, an entire forest; he would sing woeful old songs from his youth, songs sung by topmen, *Marseillaises;* there was something Russian about him, but van Gogh doesn't make clear whether it was muzhik or boyar: even the portraits seem undecided on this point. He had three children and a wife gone to wrack and ruin. What can be done with him? I look at his portraits, and while they're all contradictory, I always notice his blue sleeves, his drowning eye, and his sacred cap. Here one could say he's some sort of icon, some saint with a complicated name, Nepomucen or Chrysostom, Abbacyr mixing his flowering beard with the flowers of the sky; there he's more of a sultan with an Asshurian beard, square, brutal, but he's tired of all the bloodshed, you sense that his wide open eyes yearn to close, his soul to surrender, and his glance to turn inward to all the yellow behind him; elsewhere he comes a bit closer, holding in his laughter like my grandfather, a Chouan, a postman, or perhaps it's a day when he and the painter took one drink too many; and once he's even on the brink of the hole that all drunks fall into every evening. But everywhere there's something defenseless about him, a degree of stubbornness about his destitution, a destitution upon which he had grown cozily dependent; there's his inspirited, startled gaze, the sort usually given to a minor character in a Russian novel who's forever hesitating between the Heavenly Father and the nearby bottle, rationalizing their combination by some strange casuistry, leaning toward one and then the Other, interchanging them without a second thought; but always he's the devoted muzhik, the grumbler, driving his boyar's sled onward with strong prayers and mild impieties, the sleigh bells jingling: and this pale lord bundled up in back, wearing astrakhan and red beard—it's van Gogh—rich by chance and quiet by nature, riding beneath the fat sun of a Mother Russia that he doesn't paint. Sure, postman Roulin could drive a sleigh—but he could also ride in back, a less distinguished boyar, though more robust than the redhead; amongst growling trains in Saint-Charles station, he could open a big bag that swallows up the daily mail and find no letters to him and then grumble about his luck and the trains; or, just as easily, he could be tinkering in a Melvillean foretop, accumulating gripes against his captain's madness, but sympathetic and understanding underneath it all; and I also see him standing in front of paintings in the yellow house, agape, neither for nor against, tolerant and unconvinced: because he doesn't know anything about Art, so how could he teach us anything? Beneath his tolerance or his doubt, we don't know what there is. He's a character of little help when one is foolish enough to write about painting. But he suits me. He appears exhausted, but he could be as lively as his shape. He's as empty as a rhythm. This hollow scansion, an inner rhythm of language, inflexible and deaf, that strangles what one is struggling to say, feeds it and fatigues it—I want it to bear his name; so that words and the rhythms of language instantly endorse the great peacoat and hat of the post office; so that words and their rhythms grow old in Marseille and remember Arles; so that words end up sprouting beards; they'll appear in Prussian blue; they'll be alcoholic and republican; they won't make sense of one drop of the paintings; but with some luck, or by kidnapping, perhaps words will once again become a painting; they'll be muzhik or boyar as the spirit moves me—and completely arbitrary, as usual—but will come visibly to light, manifest, and die.

JOSEPH ROULIN OUTLIVED VAN GOGH by quite some time.

I assume he received several letters from Saint-Rémy. And as usual their writer—as when writing to the brother, Théo, who had money, or to Gauguin, or Guillaumin and Bernard, all of whom had a knack for painting, something he did not have—said not that things were improving but that things would improve; not that he was painting well but that he would: the great despair, the cockroaches floating like black ideas in his soup, the unconditional surrender to the benign and ferocious hands of Charcot's disciples—these things were simply the fault of wind and circumstance, of the poorly supplied paint-seller, of Delacroix's yellow that was so hard to get right, of nerves; but never due to the fact that one is, uncompromisingly, Vincent van Gogh. How would Roulin have read them? Certainly not as I read them, not this conniving and inaccurate reading that we're all guilty of, so very interpretive, as if each phrase were meant as a final polite gesture to destiny, as if, without any illusions, they were written to Hope herself: "It's a difficult time," they read; "It's wind and circumstance"; and we don't want to believe them, to take their word for it; we know that beneath their words they're spinning out of control, beyond salvation; we've become arrogant since we learned that all language lies. We've learned the worst and have gotten used to it. For Roulin, it wasn't quite so simple: the letters made him think; think as when one doesn't read between the lines, but reads the lines themselves; when one simply wants to believe what is written; when you work for the post office at the end of the last century. Therefore, idyllically, I imagine him handling van Gogh's letters in his kitchen, opening them; reading them word by word, attempting to envision the things and events described clearly before his eyes: the Saint Paul Hospice in Saint-Rémy; the little room with pale gray-green wallpaper and two sea green curtains; the madness, a sickness like any other (why not, we say the same of the clap, odd as that might seem); and outside, the fields of wheat. When the other frolicked in metaphor, he frowned a little, lifting his head, looking at the portraits of Gambetta or Blanqui (or why not someone a little more radical, younger, or even someone executed, like Rossel or Rigault—none of them would have been absent from a wall in his kitchen): once again he thought that the beaux arts and politics were complicated things; but then he would smile, starting over, with a satisfied little laugh that made Mother Roulin raise her head from her corner and, making the most of this attention, say: "It seems to be going better, he's gotten back his taste for living"; or: "Anyway, he did two paintings the day before yesterday. But the mistral is really bothering him." This was when he wasn't drunk. Because when he had been drinking, one duke or another—Tonkin or Grevy—was suddenly to blame for having sunk both Rivière's gunboats and Vincent's sanity in the same great hole government malfeasance always seems to dig; and he cried while thinking about the road on the outskirts of Arles where they would settle beneath the plane trees in the morning, one to paint and the other to chat, when life was less dear and people were of better spirits, when one was elsewhere. So he received letters from Saint-Rémy. But none from Auvers, because his boyar got too carried away toward the end, his sleigh, sans muzhik, flying toward the polders of his youth, the tombs of Zundert; Vincent made too recklessly for the black within the golden trumpets, too recklessly to dare or to deign to pretend any hope for himself by corresponding. So no letters from Auvers. After about a year, Roulin began to worry about this silence; after two or five, he wrote to Théo, whom he called Monsieur Gogh, as is borne out by the letters he sent him: he didn't know that the two brothers, after having dueled for years with toy swords, were to end up felled by the same blow, and that Théo, the charitable brother, guilty and tyrannical, had waited barely three years to follow the cracked brother who, in a way, was his boyar as well; so he too filled himself with lead and was laid to rest beside Vincent, whence no letters would come; maybe next he wrote to Monsieur Paul, the topman, *le casseur d'assiettes* whom he had also known in Arles, but the address had changed; *le casseur d'assiettes* had been broken like the rest. Paul Gauguin went softly to sleep in the Marquesas, where neither our tongues nor our letters can follow. Finally, one day, his letters to Vincent were returned with a note that I'd like to believe was signed by Adeline Ravoux, the daughter of a hotel owner from Auvers whom Vincent had painted in the flower of her youth, also in blue, but in cobalt, not in the Prussian blue of Roulin; this little Adeline whom he'd perhaps desired at the end simply because she had been around, whose blue dress was perhaps the vision he took with him, as they say, for certainly it was she who had taken care of him in the smoke-filled attic during the most lamentable two days of agony the world has ever known, as he burned pipe after pipe without stopping until his death, as the witnesses confirm, while above this morbid smoking room the sun beat down upon Auvers. In this letter she said: "Monsieur Vincent killed himself while he was lodging with us"; she didn't say: "In the wheat fields"; she didn't say: *sur le motif.* She didn't know how to write this novel that has been written too often ever since. She added that he had been buried there, in Auvers, and that gentlemen from Paris had come.

Therefore, one day, the big Saint-Charles train brought this letter, and it fell into his bag at the very end of the Mediterranean Line. Roulin read the young girl's words; and maybe it was early in April of '93 when the sky expands and unfolds from Estaque to Cassis and one's spirit is as fresh as the leaves of a plane tree; when the day is full of promise; it was *Chez Jean Marie* or *A la Demi-Lune,* bistros where you might have a morning glass of white. His wine in front of him, he read these words and learned of a downfall that shocked him no more than had Badinguet's, but that pained and perhaps revolted him as much as the recent topple of rebellious, red-scarved youths, falling in groups at the wall of *Père-Lachaise,* under machine-gun fire, in this Paris he didn't know. That Vincent had fallen too? He wasn't shocked at all.

The Life of Joseph Roulin

He had been undergoing such shocks for so long that they had sunk into his skin and wouldn't leave, so he kept them hidden beneath the little veil of alcohol and his postal routine, just as he kept his balding head hidden beneath his hat; these shocks, however, remained unchanged, remained juvenile, without his even knowing it; and without even knowing that it was astonishment he was feeling, which is to say emptiness—the fear of this emptiness and the taste for that fear—he had placed his convictions behind barriers like absinthe and his cap. And it's time we talk more about these shocks.

He was born in Lambesc, not far from Arles, near the middle of the century. I have never been there; they tell me that it's one of those desolate places right off a highway where you happen to stop and eat a slice of leathery pizza, and you see nothing but a dusty sky, a few people on a street, a vague dome that shines in the background, decapitated plane trees in the fore—nothing. No doubt little has changed. Still, it's a place that figures in his memories. It's the place of his childhood, and from it he must carry with him memories of almonds he swiped, or of the derelict house that was a haunt for runagate kids, or of the earliest emotions that were overlooked, once or several times, that got mixed all together in one head with the memories of the living silhouette, the rage and the red beard of a man as massively notable today—and perhaps for as few reasons—as the Manhattan skyline. There, in Lambesc, nothing had shocked him; or, if you prefer, everything had, ever since he was a very young child: the name of Eugenie de Montijo, Empress; the Algerian infantrymen on parade; perhaps the rooster's cry; father clutching mother close; the great ochre facades exposing themselves to the sky; the cymbals atop the slanting veils trailing a hearse—memories of all that is brutal and delectable. And it was no more of a shock to be promised to a minor occupation, to have to earn a living, and to have to lose it someday, and face it all honorably, cheerfully, as if it were all just tinkering in a forecastle. The time came when he let his beard grow. Perhaps an uncle pulled some strings and he joined the Post Office, and there he wasn't even a postman, as legend tells us and I amuse myself to imagine, not a mail carrier, but a desk clerk, or more precisely, a guard, something like a custodian for the mail that the trains unload in the stations of Arles and Marseille.

There—when a young sultan's beard was beginning to grow, when he was still a little uncomfortable in the big peacoat and fringed cap that weren't really designed for his gestures, for his body that hadn't yet become the liturgical second skin, dalmatic or pschent, that one now sees in the holy sanctuaries of Boston or New York—he underwent his first shock (and of course it was, in fact, his second, because at about the same time he'd had the surprise of the female body first unveiled, its massive appearance, its weight; it happened near the exit of a dance hall in Lambesc, in Rognes or Saint-Cannat, at night beneath a tree, lifting up a skirt interminably, trembling, or maybe in a whorehouse where everything is stripped away and given in one shot, but, of course, one trembles less; and it doesn't really matter here, because that surprise is universal. It matters no more to me than does that other trembling—the fissure of light penetrating the soul, striking once and for all the first cymbals of alcohol, as high and strong as those in the sky: but this too is a commonplace). I think that what surprised him, while his beard was growing and while, little by little, his body was becoming the Prussian blue peacoat, was the idea of the Republic, the eternal republican utopia, whatever name one might choose to give it; and if someone had asked him what about it had fascinated him since his youth, since he had developed the means or the curiosity to study a little and to think for himself, he would have responded with the eternal radical arguments; he would have said that he only wanted this: that men have dealings without spitefulness, or at least without the spitefulness that usually is the bread of their dealings, as if Cain's were a Mother Goose tale, as if both words and teeth weren't made to bite, the value of money were not the only thing people could see, as if other things were visible, were valued as highly; that bread be broken each day across the Earth in a perpetual Eucharist, with everyone cast as both messiah and apostle, where there was no Judas; that the last became the first, and a postman's cap a crown amongst all others. He would have responded this way and he would have been lying. Because what he loved about this idea that he couldn't acknowledge was that, nourished by it, he could leap outside the law: when he walked toward the postal wagon with his heavy stride, when he heavily opened the door that creaked on its hinges, when he bent docilely as his shoulders received the weight of the mailbags, trudging under it—all the while, watching him work and fooling around right next to him, there was another Roulin, unburdened, clandestine, and idle, a prince Roulin whose beard was perfumed and whose youth was eternal, wearing a sky blue frogged-dolman and a simple naval officer's cap that the princes wore out of modesty or to affect a more casual air. And this unburdened prince—who fluttered around him while he toiled, who burst into easy laughter when Roulin got bawled out, trumpeting in the notes of absinthe and charging like a soldier while a *Marseillaise* resonated impeccably—the world simply did not want him; the world did not see him; he was off-limits and invisible, perhaps as incomprehensible as the idea of the republic itself. And Roulin enjoyed this prohibition, this little outlaw prince who lived within him. He had grown up under the rule of the Empire during an era when the republic was truly off-limits; when later it was instituted for good and was in some way compulsory, he decided once again that it hadn't yet arrived, because when it was declared, when it had a clear president and a clear flag, prince Roulin still remained invisible; therefore, the day when the playful prince would finally, patently appear, probably with red flag in hand, ready to leave the old clothes of the old Roulin behind, was put off indefinitely, until the sun would rise in the West, until the *Grand Soir*. I wonder if the postman had really wanted that advent, because he knew too well that this frolicsome prince was also ferocious; he had a taste for vengeance, and so it happened that at the end of Roulin's long days of humiliation the prince would appear in Roulin's kitchen, forever young, but no longer larking about, his face long like a day without bread, pale, romantic, contrived, impeccably topped by Fouquier-Tinville's great, black-plumed hat, and above the weary head of mother Roulin, who didn't see this prince, he would read the names of another cartload of people sentenced to death. The republic was something ferocious: and that he loved this impeccable savagery, this promise of black plumes, and of names to cross out of existence—that, above all, is what long ago had upset good little Roulin.

You don't have to be a sorcerer to figure out how it had

happened, what precarious forms it had assumed while becoming imbedded within him: the image of Gavroche frozen in midair, either rising or falling, and the high barricade and little rosette, all in a tattered book; the name *les Trois Glorieuses;* the heroic rumors of blue-collar resolve halting the great charge of the cuirassiers, the white coats of the workers and the red flags of the others standing watch through the night, face-to-face, trembling; the memory of his father's humiliations, in whom, perhaps, a prince with black feathers and a sky blue cap had also reigned; the brochures in which unremembered hacks had appeared—Anacharsis Cloots and possibly the others, the Brutuses who were locked up in '93—those who had seized their hour of princedom between two eras of executions, those exultant lawyers whom he took for members of the proletariat, like himself. And, of course, there was a young Blanquiste with white hands, perhaps with a red beard, a broken-down boyar who, in his cheap room, spoke feverishly in incomprehensible words describing an incomprehensible paradise flowing with rivers of blood. And the young Roulin, who didn't dare demand explanations, simply opined wisely, listening petrified while this ferocity resonated long within him; and this ferocity, doubtless the same that pushed him into the white pit of absinthe, this rage, or this fear, became concrete, took flag and song, even took shape and joined the visible world.

So much for the republic. Its shadow was the only thing that helped him to refuse to be Roulin, which is to say, to accept pretending to be Roulin; this denial dressed him each morning in the great peacoat, brutally pushed him before daybreak toward the mail bags and the reprimands, but as if it were someone else at work. The prince was either larking or being massacred in some recess of the postman, who was just going through the motions. This gave him an inner life, and with it, he married Augustine, in whom he sowed his seed; he cajoled and reprimanded Armand, Camille, and Marcelle, all issue of Augustine; he made a little garden in which to grow lettuce. It gave him a cover, because it isn't enough in this world just to be a postman, or a storekeeper— as if that weren't murderous enough: you have to declare yourself a postman for the red or the white, to have ideas and a jumble of hackneyed words and attitudes that one calls a personality; you need these little trifles so you don't drink your absinthe alone in a bistro on the outskirts of Arles, so that you're not singled out, so that you don't slip into the gutter. All this led him to the age of forty-seven years and the appearance that the paintings reveal. And then we have to believe that he was surprised a second time.

PERHAPS IT WAS IN SOME BISTRO, or more precisely at the *Café de la Gare, place Lamartine,* chez Mother Ginoux, the beautiful hotel proprietress who was painted wearing a little lace bonnet and a black shawl, her hand pensive and weary, her eye imperial and weary, painted as few Spanish queens had been, as if, without hesitation, the great Spaniards themselves had descended to guide the hand of the painter. Her husband had also been painted, next to the long, empty billiard table, beneath the gas-burning lamps, in hell, more spectre than king of Spain, insubstantial, insomniac, and pale. It was in this same hell or good haven that on one October night, the dead king received Monsieur Paul, who was coming to join Monsieur Vincent, a bag slung over his shoulder with the odd bearing of a sailor, a topman, Monsieur Paul about whom he'd heard so much that he recognized him instantly, whom he therefore welcomed, proudly guiding him around the tables of what Vincent called *dormeurs petits,* little sleepers, toward a table near the hearth, and then served him a grog with all the attention and kindness only the living are capable of. Or, perhaps, it was at the church square, which is also *place de la République,* blessed by the massive crucifix of Saint Trophime, which Roulin didn't care about, but where the tricolor billowed, and he did care about that. Perhaps it was there, at high noon, thanks to the Zouave who knew both of them from somewhere else, who put them face-to-face in broad daylight and with excited, inexact words, introduced them, his enormous red culotte spread between the two as they eyed each other. Or it was near the gas works, or *pont Langlois,* amidst the modernism of the high furnaces or the archaism of running water; or perhaps, inevitably, along the melancholy Alyscamps. And it was simply at the train station, at the end of a very hot afternoon in June or July, when the postman was on duty, say, working at the dispatch desk for the fourth-class mail deposit, *la petite vitesse,* sitting in a stifling little room, slouching a little, staring at his shoes, sick of being Joseph Roulin and having to wear such enormous boots in this heat. Raising his head, he saw a client in front of him on the other side of the window. The customer wasn't wearing the yellow hat; his hair wasn't shaved short; he wasn't gesturing madly; he wasn't sputtering incomprehensibly; he didn't appear mad, and he was smaller than the Manhattan skyline; he had an accent that we don't know, but a red beard that we do, and he wore a blue thrift-shop suit made of denim or drugget. He handed the postman a package he wished to send by way of *la petite vitesse* to a Monsieur Théodore van Gogh, living in Paris; the package was long, cylindrical, rather heavy, and on the form in the section marked "Content of Parcel" he wrote that it was paintings. The postman was surprised that they could roll up and wander off, just like that, without the golden frames from which they seem inseparable, that give them dignity and rigor. So of course they started talking, because the postman was curious, because he thought he knew that the republic—the true Republic, not the one that had just usurped the tricolor to colonize Tonkin and nourish the Jesuits, but the other one in which, in his dreams, he was a Prince—loved the beaux arts and functioned in such a way that everyone involved with the beaux arts had a chance at a just reward, in which they could find a pleasure in their trade as unambiguous as absinthe, instead of the shame that comes from appreciating none of it and having to pretend to understand it all; and van Gogh, who in the end got nothing from the beaux arts or from those he met, was drawn violently toward them both all the same. So they begin talking and find that they enjoy each other's company; Roulin gets up, they leave, they cross *place Lamartine,* which is all yellow; the smaller of the two stops in front of a house even more yellow, pointing it out to Roulin, who stands in polite amazement, nodding his head, taking a step as if to go inside but the first holds him back, the renovations aren't finished, it's too soon to go inside for a drink; the two of them stand there for an instant, they hesitate, they float, between the yellow roughcast earth and the pure cobalt sky; the great Manichaean and Byzantine terrains of reality have been confronted; then they leave again, both in Prussian blue, Roulin bigger, more visible, more bearded; beside him the other's head is bowed, solitary, attentive, something aristocratic in the way he closes the flap on a pocket or grasps firmly the collar of his drugget coat; Roulin looks at him out of the corner of his eye, the striped arm of the peacoat pushes open a glass-paneled door, allowing the other to go in first, the artist—enter my prince—and at last the boyar and his muzhik are in a good haven, in hell; they sit down in the *Café de la Gare* surrounded by the clashing green and red decor, Manichaean, old Russian, and within this oven they smile at each other and turn their eyes in unison toward the little green Louis XV counter over there, and behind it stands something like a queen of Spain, an Arlesienne; they take out their pipes, share their tobacco. Marie Ginoux serves their bocks.

There they are the next day, face-to-face in the yellow house studio that no one can describe; the walls themselves can tell us nothing, having been razed to the ground by American bombs falling from the pure cobalt in 1944. From the paintings, however, we know that the walls were white limestone, which is to say that van Gogh painted them whatever color suited him, and that the tiles underfoot were red, because he always painted them red. So it's there that Roulin became a painting, matter less mortal than flesh, all in this shack that today is as invisible and well known as the Manhattan skyline; or perhaps it was in his house, the postman's, today unknown, tucked away, and withdrawn within the only ineffable memory that the walls could hold, but that we know lay between the two railroad bridges, and so there it would be, had the American meteors not destroyed it too; in this house that lies between the two railroad bridges, vibrating, proletarian, smoky, or in the yellow house that looks out upon oleander bushes and plane trees, the house where he once again hoped as he hadn't since Zundert, the house he privately referred to as the artists' co-op, like a new *Salon des Indépendants;* he swept and bleached it clean, bustling about all summer, transforming crates into furniture, hanging paintings of sunflowers and Chinese ornaments to make it look nice, a small washbowl on the night table and a hand towel on the wall for washing up; there, once, raising his head to look at the studio, he stood weeping for joy, a sandwich in his hand; there, with his arms raised skyward, he welcomed Gauguin, worked with Gauguin, argued with Gauguin, and there, to finish things off, he came home drunk and alone on a night bereft of cicadas or a Messiah, December 24, cut off his ear as we know, and did with it what we know, finally falling into the remains of the washbowl and, oblivious, slept as outside slept the rosebays without roses, the black plane trees. In one of these two houses, one by one, he painted each of the members of this holy, proletariat family just like the Other, generous and long suffering; this holy family that offered him jams, wine, and the simple joys of family Sundays that chase death away, welcoming him with open arms, perhaps to piss off the neighbors, but more probably just because they loved him; in return, all of them appear on the little canvases now scattered throughout capitals of the globe far from Arles, given as examples to the living, not because of the preserves they offered long ago, but because of the painting. He painted Armand at seventeen, fighting with his father, wanting to join the army—he would rather have died than work for the post office like his father—preferring to do nothing with his life, wanting to embark gloriously down the great roads of the world that lead everywhere except Arles, wanting to leave; Armand Roulin, whose jaw was a bit effete, who had his father's flat nose, and already in his eyes, at the temples, the same veil as his father, the one from absinthe and hopeless revolts; the young rebel also failed due to wind and circumstance, ending up much later in Tunisia as what van Gogh called an *officier de paix* and while he was there realizing that the great roads go everywhere but Tunisia, living a bad dream, exploiting the Arabs and playing Russian roulette with the wind, dying there, and it wasn't a dream, his portrait hanging in Rotterdam not marking the blow in any way, not a hair is out of place, and of course it didn't fall off the wall on November 24, 1945; Armand-Joseph-Désiré, proud with no reason to be, but whom the redhead made look quite dignified and justifiably proud, as if smitten with etiquette and points of honor, with a white tie and a mimosa yellow jacket, sullen and ephebe like a general of the Empire, chic as a Manet, a baron from the *Café d'Athènes,* a son of Spain; van Gogh made him look quite dignified, but in van Gogh's own way, which is to say both muddy and gleaming, *rastacouère.* He also painted the youngest child, poor Camille, who was but unsound dust in a schoolboy's cap, enveloped in royal blue, bathing in the crimson of a wall; and in the crimson, muddy; and Augustine with little Marcelle in her arms, the bundle of dirty linen born in July, sprung from Roulin's seed, whom he baptized without a priest, in his own way, as republicans do; and Augustine again, alone, a Roulin *née* Pellicot, whom van Gogh called *cell qui berce,* the one who cradles, massive, sentimental, as old as the roads, as if singing to herself in her isba on the outskirts of Arles for distant topmen, her clayey hands clasped in prayer, but her face neat and glowing against the Veronèse dahlias, thousandfold blooms, the same celestial pasture as Abbacyr, her holy husband. And to the fanatic who painted them, Armand would talk about the great big world in which he would leave his mark when he left this jumping-off point, Augustine spoke of Armand and her worries about his future, Camille said nothing, and little Marcelle stood awkwardly braced against the future, clenching her little fists, crying. But it was the father he painted most often, in the ways I've described, with his attributes, the hat and the beard, the blue sleeves, his temple lightly brushed by drunkenness and the wing of the Republican angel, as if absent, but looming. And the father, who couldn't keep still during the sessions, would come peer over Vincent's shoulder, bursting into laughter or scowling, busy as a muzhik, but tiring, the father, very surprised, watching himself being painted by this red son fallen from the sky.

What surprised him isn't in any of the books. It wasn't Vincent's originality, his eccentricities; he'd read the newspapers, he knew that artists were a strange breed; and besides, he himself was original, a turbulent presence within a neighborhood that took him for a radical: so the yellow hat, the lively fits, his way of speaking ornately—it was all to be expected. It wasn't that he was any more miserable than the others; those same newspapers had unveiled that the artist in his thirties is usually poor, that it adds to his vigor, to his seriousness, adds to the éclat of his revenge when he finally triumphs, and gives him a clear conscience that acts as proof of his self-resolve; and we know what misery is all about, how to deal with it, how to charm it with bits of magic, the preserves, the wine, the Sunday dinners; and if underneath it all the artist is somehow a proletarian, as the leftist papers affirm, then to nourish him is a pious act. It wasn't about being chosen as a model by a painter from Paris—why not him? He was just as worthy as anyone else. It wasn't even van Gogh's painting in itself, the finished products in which Roulin saw himself become someone else, tolerant and unconvinced, noticing that his beard was too green or too curly, or here as inflexible as justice miscarried, his eye sultanlike or saintly, and his hat—always well rendered: all in all, he must not have found it very pretty and must have told him so or, more probably, just kept it to himself, because he had an open mind and knew that Monsieur Vincent knew what he was doing. And of course, within this Dutchman who was gentle most of the time, filled with caring attentions and gratitude, there was also a fierce prince that the sort of prince in Roulin had noticed right away, perhaps in the same way that Vincent had watched Mother Ginoux undulate her way around the tables when she brought them their bocks, in the same way that within his courteous words would sometimes resonate an uncompromising order, in the way that he always painted: his was only a more decorated prince, more imperious and better born than Roulin's, something different from a postman's prince, the equal of a man who had traveled and knew several languages; the equal of a boyar. And Roulin regretted that such violent appetites had been locked into a man so agonizingly unlucky; Roulin knew all this in his own way, accepted it without surprise, and loved him with a touch of duplicity, fraternally.

Let's look at Roulin one Sunday morning in August, following the fanatic down a road on the outskirts of Arles, when it wasn't portraits that he was painting but when he went *sur le motif,* thus preparing the work of his biographers, doing the solar-liturgy thing, the Mexican standoff with the source of all light; and there, I'm sure he saw nothing liturgical or Mexican, but something pictorial, yes, and audacious, since he was doing what the Impressionists themselves seldom dared do; if he was wearing the yellow hat, it was simply because the sun was beating down; neither Roulin nor I see anything sacrificial about it. So there it is: there they are, fairly far along the road to Tarascon; they descend into a great field of melons or wheat billowing down below; the cicadas are tirelessly devouring time, space, as it's already ten o'clock; van Gogh could have managed without Roulin, he tries not to see or hear him, but he doesn't make him leave—he's a good man to be with when not painting; he plants the easel, he takes out the three chrome yellow tubes, squeezes one of them and applies it, and once again the little drama hesitates and unfolds on a canvas for the biographers to come, the businessmen in Manhattan; Roulin sits beneath a tree, perhaps with a small picnic basket and a bottle from Augustine beside him, and he watches. He had tried to gab a little, but he quickly shut up, the other answering halfheartedly, out of his head and in a hurry, looking at the fields of melons and some meagre lumps in the distance, the foothills of the Alps, as if all the little made-up ladies from *rue des Récollettes* were dancing and lifting their skirts, leaping toward him, calling to him, denying him; Roulin looks at the great expanse before the foothills, twenty kilometers at least—and of course he knows neither who created them nor to what end, why the wheat grows there and later yellows, why one time out of two the sun up above replaces the stars—but he knows the names of the people who live on the farms, which families withdraw into the shade to elude the sun's rays and with the sun's help grow their wheat; he knows who built the little surrounding wall, how long it takes to go by foot to Montmajour, which you can see from here; he knows that at Fontvieille, which you can't see, lying hidden by those cypresses, is a republican confrere whose company he enjoys. The cicadas sing louder, from tree to tree, covering the visible world. And before this expanse that one needn't name—which is clearly marked on cadastres, the wheat of which will be fairly distributed to the less fortunate when the true republic finally cloisters the world—Roulin now watches this man of meagre volume, standing and preoccupied, incomprehensible, who doesn't even know the names of these places and in lieu of the cadastral marks applies thick yellows and perfunctory blues to a canvas of meagre dimensions, a fabric of unreadable runes more aware of the hills than of Roulin, scorning him more than those foothills would if you were hiking them and midday sneaked up on you, without a tree in sight. I would like to believe that once again he is surprised; I hope what surprises him is a question perhaps as imposing, perhaps as superfluous as and even more opaque than the future of the human race, which, in his own words, he called the republic; the question that played through him and that certainly never made it into words, but in which he exalted, filling him with a great pity for, and devotion to, the painter, is this: Roulin asked himself by what ruse more perverse than the seizure of the notaries during the Republic of '93, by what outlandishness painting seemed to him, and actually was, a human occupation like any other—carrying as its burden the need to represent what is seen, as others are burdened with raising wheat or making money beget money, an occupation that is learned and passed on, producing tangible things destined to make the houses of the rich look nice, or to be placed in churches to exalt the devoted little souls of the children of Mary, or in the prefectures to call young men to a career, the army, the Colonies—how and why this occupation, useful and clear, had become this phenomenal anomaly, despotic, dedicated to nothing, empty, this catastrophic labor that, on its passage between a man and the world, had tossed to one side the carcass of the redhead, starving, without honor, running straight for the bedlam and knowing it—and to the other had thrown landscapes left formless from the force of thought, and unrecognizable faces wanting perhaps but to resemble the man, all in a world streaming with uninhabitable shapes, with stars burning too hot and water in which to drown. Behind the field of melons, horsemen of the Camargue march past, cowboys far from Hollywood; they're all in black, their hats and their lances, since the road is black beneath the oaks; van Gogh isn't painting them, he's into chrome yellow number three, the pure sun; he sweats; in his own way, Roulin is rethinking the enigma of the beaux arts.

It should be said that Roulin was in good hands: before his eyes was a mirage more powerful than that of the *Grand Soir.* He had before him in the little fields of melons, at the Sunday dinner table and on the bowling greens of *place Lamartine,* a piece of abstraction made flesh, the incarnation of the theory of the beaux arts as the romantics had concocted, that the other schools had affirmed, and that still has a hold on us today, a product manufactured by books that managed to survive, but suffered; someone who had believed so devotedly in this theory that he had become theory himself, ascended to almost the same height, and died of it. And Roulin, who didn't know the theory but saw its unmistakable incarnation, was astonished; because you don't see that kind of thing every day; the same way that before the Knight of La Mancha, Sancho asked himself some questions; the same way that the apostles were spellbound before the other Incarnation, the one whose theory was thousands of years in the works, whose pages became flesh in the melon fields of Judah, named and marked on cadastres as well: because no one is more sensitive to the book made man, they say, than those who don't read books. And that's enough: Joseph Roulin, who didn't really know anything about the beaux arts and who, all in all, didn't find van Gogh's painting very pretty, appreciated all of it as if he had perceived that the arts from the end of this century, Art as they say, adds to the opacity of the world, troubling its all too credulous servants, all the way to the grave, in a violent dance, perhaps lively and ferocious, whose meaning fails to surface.

That's why, in front of his glass of white wine, in a bistro of *la Joliette,* Roulin wasn't shocked to read words written in the indecisive handwriting of a young girl: "Monsieur Vincent killed himself when he was with us." But then he wasn't thinking about painting, about the incarnation of a theory, or about the pompous concoctions in which, fairly obscurely, he believed—in which we all believe. He thought about a client's accent in the Arles train station during an afternoon in June, about the white tablecloths in the Carrel restaurant, the aioli, Vincent's laugh when he sang the *Marseillaise* over dessert; he thought about the whole thing with the ear, how he hadn't been allowed—him, Roulin—to go into the hospital room right away, but that Augustine had been allowed to, and he, waiting outside in the hallway, had seen her come out crying; he thought perhaps of a line from the letter he wrote the next day to Monsieur Gogh: "Yesterday, Thursday, my wife went to see him and he hid his face when he saw her come in." Because in these stories about art, there are also the ultimate moments of shame of the great red children.

Let's have a last look at Arles through the fingers van Gogh places over his face, when he had once again botched a painting, or when he awoke December 25 and saw the gendarmes, the hand towel filled with blood, the broken washbowl; when he saw Mother Roulin come in whom nonetheless he had painted. Let's look at Arles where there's the little *pont Langlois,* so tender and blue, an even bluer sky; *vaqueros;* zouaves; a copy of the *Forum républicain* where you read on the third page that a Foreigner cut off his own ear and brought it to a whore; a petition left at the town hall, signed by a neighborhood that wants to lock up a man who doesn't have all of his head, in which I hope with all my strength that the name of Mother Ginoux does not figure, the name of the queen of Spain; fields of wheat or melons and an old, infallible sun. We are leaving. We are not leaving Europe, as Armand Roulin will quite soon, and we remain on this earth that van Gogh has already abandoned. We are going to Marseille, with the great peacoat and cap of the post office, on a body growing old.

MARSEILLE IS NEARER TO THE SUN than Arles. Van Gogh— who never thought as far as Rome, who was too modest or barbaric to think that far—van Gogh had thought about Marseille throughout his life; I don't know what novel had made him imagine it to be some sort of artists' Mecca, as he'd said, but he was surely the only artist to think it so, all because the painter Monticelli had lived and died there—done in by arrogance, misery, and absinthe, a painter he ranked as highly as Rembrandt, Rubens, Delacroix—Monticelli whose paintings I wouldn't know how to judge but that they tell me aren't so ugly; all Manhattan's gold didn't come bail him out, and on some shadowy provincial grave, tourists read a name that means nothing to them, he is lost: perhaps he wasn't radical enough; he wasn't friends with Pissarro, Seurat, those of the *beau monde;* and, of course, he's missing the blow from the Browning *sur le motif* and the massive psychiatric syndrome; or—if God had not forsaken us—he didn't know how to paint a proprietress as a queen of Spain, nor the first verses of the first book in a wheatfield, while the sunlight yellows. So van Gogh wanted to go to Marseille with Gauguin, and they would have gone there if, after two months in the yellow house, they hadn't come to blows about wind and circumstance, overcooked onions, or each of their supercilious failures; and they would have strolled along the Canebière in full regalia, straight out of a picture postcard and so decked-out that Vincent would have written about it to Théo—immense yellow hat, not the straw but some kind of Stetson, black velvet jacket and white pants, yellow gloves, a reed cane and the air of a southern gentleman; and who knows if this would only have been a picture postcard, if it should make us smile: who knows if a rich van Gogh wouldn't have been as elegant as Manet, and just as smitten with etiquette. But he never made it there: and, postmortem, he delegated Roulin.

Great castles of canvas are still entering the *Vieux Port* of this era, Melville's very own; there are sailors and provisions, insatiable hungers, knife wounds; the sea opens up beyond Joliette's docks and straight across, on the other side, is Egypt, whence came the arts and the merchants, the plague; where there are towers as tall as Manhattan's own, and in their padlocked basements, kings turned to ashes settled in gold, golden, as everywhere beneath the towers. Standing around the *Vieux Port*, Roulin doesn't think about any of this; he considers a spot where the world passes by en masse, Sundays or early on a weekday morning; he's thinking about Armand, who's on the other side of the same sea, sweating the natives for gold; maybe he's thinking about the radiant tomorrows for the proletariats of Valparaiso, Alexandria, Piraeus, where commodities of every color and every language will debark before their eyes, maybe even some paintings, the holy commodity; and this prince Roulin—decorated like an officer of Montenegro, but invisibly—is moved, forever young in a Roulin who is no longer. Then he turns his back on this restlessness and returns through the plane trees; nineteen-year-old girls sell oysters beneath the leaves; he sings that *le temps des cerises* has returned, but not for him, he must hurry; he doesn't work here; he works at the train station where other commodities bustle about, but none of the holy commodity that was rolled up and sent to Théo, a station that may already be called Saint-Charles, at the top of those interminable stairs; and he labors to climb them.

After the letter from the little Ravoux, for ten years or more, he didn't hear any news of van Gogh. He wasn't expecting any. But in their kitchen—from which Armand had fled for the Colonies in the white tie and yellow vest we'll imagine him wearing no matter what his age; the kitchen that Camille deserted as well, the child made from unsound dust that nonetheless a sea-freight shipping company, the *Messageries maritimes,* had taken under its wing and paid meagrely each month, so that he'd work in a dismal bonded warehouse in Toulon or Cassis with others as unsound as he; the same kitchen where the tense young man had always appeared for Roulin alone, behatted after Fouquier, or, on more carefree days, with a sky blue cap; the kitchen where Marcelle was still within earshot and in their arms, weaker than when she was two months old and braced against the future, already wasting away, silently; in their kitchen, therefore, perhaps hung with cheap Veronèse wallpaper with fat dahlias, a celestial pasture, the muzhik and his baba spoke of Vincent from time to time. Newspapers reported, for example, the opening of the *Salon,* and they thought about how proud he would have been to be there, the poor guy: to go, he would have to have rented a stovepipe hat and a swallow-tailed coat, and they laughed imagining him in that get-up, boarding the train for Paris; or perhaps Augustine, while cleaning, found a letter, either from Monsieur Gogh or Monsieur Paul, from before he'd lost his marbles or afterward—she and Roulin didn't agree. They argued about it a little. Mother Roulin felt sorry for him, slowly nodding her head with conviction, and Roulin, who was only listening out of one ear, envisioned all that effort spent for nothing in the fields of Arles, thrown to the wind, as violent and inconsequential as the passing of cowboys on horseback, in the shadows of the oak trees, at noon. They asked themselves what had become of the paintings, paintings that weren't very pretty, but had cost so much suffering; at least at their house such pain had been in some way rewarded; at least one of these paintings had been unrolled and mounted in a handsome golden frame with large moldings that they themselves had chosen; one out of all of those things thrown furiously to the wind had been hung, and few of the world's eyes had seen it there, as one sees the great work of the great painters at the *Salon,* and it was in their home, in their kitchen, between the chromo portrait of Blanqui and the talking bird's cage, a blackbird or a myna, which could perhaps pronounce the names Anacharsis Cloots and Vincent van Gogh. Tolerant and unconvinced, moved, they turned their eyes to this painting I'll return to, and they looked at it for a moment. It was already the dinner hour, they were eating, and more often than not it would be the two Vincentian oblations, the yellow potato and black coffee, Vincentian from Vincent's first period that Roulin didn't know; but of the third oblation—what Vincent called *la blanche,* which we also call the green, diabolical and solar, chrome yellow number three—only Joseph partook before eating.

Sure, Roulin was still drinking; but it didn't help the way it used to. It no longer produced this desirous, violent body that the mad excesses of youth incite, this pure glory made flesh; Augustine is as old as the hills, and even the oyster girls—their sidelong glances, their white arms—if by chance or blindness they mistake you for a sultan, you would lay your hands on them in vain: nevertheless, you look at them with the same eyes you had in Lambesc, and their bodies are the same, heavy, prodigious. It seems that all the friends you drink with have changed, they've become inattentive, tactless; they no longer deign to see that beneath the postal cap something of a prince is singing and making intelligent remarks; moreover, maybe the prince speaks less willingly; there are too many things in the world that the postman hasn't understood, that he knows he'll never understand, which, therefore, the prince will no longer discuss. And on every 14th evening of July seemingly begun in good spirits—new uniform all polished, settled between the trumpets and the tricolor, the zouaves and the Algerian infantrymen, the blue sky—these nights of the taking of the Bastille you have nothing at all and end up sitting alone at a table in a bistro near the port with the black sea before you, the friends who left you to your ramblings, the young toughs who look at you and laugh with the oyster girls, the white that runs through your beard and the new uniform that you've stained, and when angrily you rise, when you push a chair and it falls, it's no longer revolt, it's no longer a down payment on the republic to come, it's the republic itself falling in this chair that you see through your stupor and something close to tears, final but somehow resembling happiness—the republic is delectably lost, fallen there, into the past; when you come home after midnight, you're just an old sot; and on an obscure back road where you stop to catch your breath, you see fireworks exploding suddenly up there like Vincent's dahlias, and you wonder, what hands gather them? What celestial herd grazes them? And then you weaken, like an old woman you say to yourself that Vincent is in the sky. You speak to him.

One day, as you might expect, van Gogh came back. It wasn't from some heart of darkness.

It's evening. Roulin has a little garden fairly far from his house, off by the wooded outskirts, here filled with tomatoes and over there some agaves, toward Estaque or Cassis; he's coming back to eat and he takes to the incline of his street, *rue Trigance* for example, toward *la Vieille Charité;* his back is to us, tired, something in his hand, peppers or endive; he's still imposing, but far more crooked than when he was pestering the fanatic with muzhiklike cabrioles on the edge of Arles. A young man who is waiting there, in a wine seller's or under an awning, watches him approach, and his face lights up as though he knows him. But Roulin has never seen this citizen before. The other moves toward him; he has a mimosa jacket and a little mustache, but it's not Armand; on his head is the inevitable steep stovepipe; he takes his hat in his hands; with a curious respect, he says a few words to the postman; at that moment, we don't see the postman's eyes, but we know that a glimmering flame dances there, because his shoulders straighten unfatigued with an air of exclamation, of gaiety that lifts his arms, opens his hands; he shows him that his house is up the road a piece, but the other already knows; together, they head up the bit of road that remains, the elegant one still with hat in hand, Roulin still wearing his cap; at the door he moves to the side—enter my prince—the young man climbs the stairs, he's upstairs. They're in the kitchen.

I want to see and hear their first conversation, in this kitchen visited and touched, for the first time, by eyes other than those of his fellow postal workers, those old nostalgic radicals from the Commune who came there to reminisce, to blaspheme; or even the eyes of Mother Roulin's neighbors, cheerful kids or old women with whom she'd go to market; but the young man wasn't looking at their kitchen because the Roulins were well liked, because they were despised, envied, or even because he wanted to chat with them and enjoy their company; his stare was the old, absent, clouded look of the prodigal son returned after ten years, after they had moved, and so he figures that, before, the buffet must have been there, and the chromo too, although he can't remember it, because now it's yellowed and dog-eared, but not this brand-new birdcage; and, no, not this bird; and Roulin understands this, barely; but that his kitchen was being scrutinized as something enormous and ancient, seen from its base, Egypt's pyramids—this Roulin doesn't understand. It doesn't matter: because what he does see clearly, what he recognizes with a blinding clarity and an extreme joy, what he hasn't seen in so long that he thought perhaps he had dreamt it, is the way the young man places himself in front of his portrait—the one that makes him look like Nepomucen in the celestial fields—the one Vincent had given him, and high time he said it, for whatever it's worth; so the young man stood there, the black hat held firmly in his hands before him, unshakable, his shoulders perfectly upright as if standing at attention before a highly decorated officer whom, of course, one would not be able to see; he remains there, on his feet, as if at the bedside of a dead man, and even so there's a tension in his lips, around his eyes, that's both ferocious and deliberate, as if upon this little framed surface there were simultaneously represented twenty kilometers of fields leading to the foothills of the Alps—thus to the end of the Earth—as well as, right within reach, a beautiful woman without shame, calling to him, about to step out from the canvas and be touched from head to toe; and nothing in it tolerant, nothing unconvinced, instead, a nonsensical intolerance and an equivalent certitude, as when remembering Gambetta's fiery rhetoric, as when you want a woman: that was how Monsieur Paul had looked at the paintings, that was how Monsieur Vincent had looked at Monsieur Paul's paintings. So this way of seeing still exists. Roulin wants to jump up, to talk a lot, but he doesn't, he understands that it's tiresome, and besides, he barely knows this young man. Here's Mother Roulin, who was out running errands; the elegant fellow seems to recognize her as well, and with good reason; and before he can say three words, leaning gently forward as one does in society, his stovepipe pressed indifferently to him, Roulin announces eagerly, "He's interested in Monsieur Vincent," and more excitedly: "He saw our portraits in Paris."

They offer him something to drink. There they are, all three of them seated around the table upon which rest a silk tophat and some muddy leeks, and in two out of three glasses there's the oblational chrome yellow number three that loosens the tongue. They're all talking, because this distinguished young man is quite chatty in his own way, like his hosts. He has just come from Arles, where he found their address, where he saw everyone, Marie Ginoux and Doctor Rey, but not the Zouave; he didn't know that the Zouave and van Gogh had been friends, moreover he might be in Tonkin, the poor guy, or at the bottom of the Yangtze, in the dead gunboats; he had been to Saint-Rémy as well, and before that to Auvers; he has seen the final room in which he knows that a pipe was smoked right up until death; he tells them this; later, he'll go to Zundert; and so here he is in Marseille: a sort of pilgrimage, in short. No, he's not related to Vincent; it's because Vincent, he tells them, is on his way to becoming a very great painter, now. Their faces light up, they talk about this for a long while. And Monsieur Paul? Monsieur Paul as well, but who knows where he is, somewhere in a Polynesia more distant than even Tonkin, he doesn't know he's becoming a great painter. He's in the Colonies, like Armand. The kitchen is full of shadow, not that it's night yet, it's the season of light, but the last of the sun is stopped by the great mass of *la Vieille Charité,* the old general hospital now serving as a barracks, right across the way. The postman has said nothing for a few moments; the beaux arts are a complicated and unexpected business, he's known this for quite some time; he is profoundly happy, he can keep quiet; a trumpet sounds from somewhere within *la Vieille Charité;* the talking bird rustles within his cage, uneasy, speaking a few halves of incomprehensible human words; in Arles, no doubt, Ginoux is lighting gas lamps in his café, Marie Ginoux descending into the main room, slowly, heavily made-up, and there below she reigns, older and more beautiful, her shawl as black as the cowboys who move off through the countryside, great fields the reaper has departed; within the diligence from Tarascon, moving too fast—and how late it is tonight, it will crush someone, it won't even stop—behind its drawn curtains, undisturbed by all the bumps, not noticing the three-franc girls at the end of *rue des Récollettes,* not looking at the yellow house on *place Lamartine,* not looking at anything between the two railroad bridges, not looking at the olive trees, not the cypresses, not looking at the little rural passersby who scatter in shock, not the risen moon, nor the postal truck tearing across *pont Langlois,* making it tremble—looking straight into the blackness behind the drawn curtains, the dead boyar, the czar, passes. Just as chez Ginoux, Mother Roulin lights a gas lamp, an old lantern she sets up on the table. Joseph's beard is broad and full, Assyrian, as before, but whiter, with a yellow still noticeable in the mustache from all the tobacco and hooch. He smiles softly; he says, "So, you too, it's painting." The other looks at him for a moment, with great sympathy and amusement; he hesitates a little; finally he says yes, him too. He puts on his hat, he has a ring, a rich stone that you notice more in lamplight than by day; he doesn't want to stay for dinner. Yes, he'll be back.

We let this young man move off. He takes big strides back down toward the dock where he has left car and driver, the country roads too narrow; the wind has picked up, so he holds his hat to his head; of course, he passes topmen and oyster girls who are now heading home; the smell of the sea is strong, all these things fill up his heart, his joy knows no bounds; he jumps into the carriage, break or trap, and just as quickly they leave: he couldn't stay for dinner, in fact; his time is limited, he wants to get to Aix tonight, and why not? There's another painter to see tomorrow, another rising myth, but this time someone very much alive, someone not devoted to the ascendant yellow note, or to the Browning; this one's tougher, has played his cards right while waiting for his hour to come. He'll have to play this hand tight. No matter. The carriage runs through the countryside, beneath the moon, and from behind the drawn curtains he looks out into the darkness before him where very clearly he imagines fabulous exhibitions for the fall, sales in New York, and a total upending in the prices of these painted things, something of which he has been one of the artisans, and not the least of them. He also sees the postman, the sultan and drunkard who recently appeared in some Parisian collections, and the other, the Saint Nepomucen or Chrysostom flanked by his talking bird, by his chromo of Blanqui. He will have this painting. He lifts a corner of the curtain, we're near Gardanne, the moon turns: and as the blackness returns, he suddenly sees Joseph Roulin with his leeks, his white beard, his ardor. He thinks about this all the way to Aix.

Roulin can't sleep either. The lantern is burning on the table. Augustine is sleeping, the myna bird too: you see only the little violent crest, yellow, an insubstantial mass balled up like a black fist. So this had been a great painter: someone whose paintings should be seen by everyone because, strangely enough, as opaque as they seem, they make things clearer, more easily understood; someone who could have been rich in the end, because these trifles command exorbitant prices. And, of course, Roulin asks himself who had decided that he was a great painter, because that didn't seem to have been decided back in Arles, and how had this transformation occurred? He looks at his framed portrait; the lantern softens the colors slightly, but you clearly see the fat dahlias and the large face that was his own. He has both his arms before him on the table; his sleeves are striped as though one had to be disguised as a marshal to lug around the mail. He looks without moving. You hear nothing outside. Vincent is sitting next to him, and he would see him were he just to glance over, but for what? He's wearing a panama and white gloves, is chic as a Manet; he is extremely calm, rejuvenated, his beard well trimmed; he's finally found the means to replace his missing teeth; and his ear—has it grown back?—or more likely it's one of those bits of flesh more real than even the flesh made in America, cardboard or painted leather; he no longer has that haughty look, the tyrannical mouth; the rage has fallen away, he's relaxed and peaceful; a few certainties make him happy, and he still paints along this certain path, and better, more slowly, more magnificently, in a great airy studio, in Paris, in a good neighborhood; and if you went to see him, there would be a lovely woman who would have you come in and sit down, more beautiful than Marie Ginoux and younger, but regal as well, and she would tell you amiably that Vincent is working, best to wait a little; she offers you newspapers, a drink. You wait; you're happy that things have turned out so well, that the catastrophic labor that had been ravaging who-knows-what on the outskirts of Arles had been forgotten, the labor thrown to the wind, wicked as lightning, that had left Vincent standing dazed before a painting where nothing appeared but a field painted in Greek. It would appear that it's no longer Greek to everyone. Roulin has taken off his hat, there's nobody there to see that he is bald, and anyway, for the moment he doesn't care: for once, the prince isn't frolicking on the outskirts, he is wholly within him; he doesn't rebel against this, he doesn't pretend to be Roulin; he is happy to be this Joseph Roulin who has seen a miracle, the transformation of Vincent into a great painter; and without a doubt he'll see the *Grand Soir* as well, that's a piece of cake, all kidding aside. Will he turn toward Vincent? No, they have nothing to say. Calmly, they look at this portrait painted long ago; and Roulin finds it almost beautiful, after all. The dahlias are blooming. From the enormous mass of *la Vieille Charité,* a peremptory note from a little trumpet is blown; it's already the reveille, perhaps. Without looking at the chair next to him, Roulin extinguishes the lantern. The flustered myna bird stirs as though speaking a name from within a dream. The old man is going to bed.

DURING THE DAYS THAT FOLLOWED, Roulin thought a lot about this young man who was off haggling with another old-timer—bearded as well, but more irascible—over the prices of various bright canvases, landscapes, portraits. He imagined the young man's passage through Arles, Arles where Roulin hadn't set foot since they had moved; maybe Ginoux had also recognized something in the young man, proudly guiding him through the groups of *dormeurs petits* to a table near the hearth, smiling and obliging beneath the infernal gas lamps; and Marie, who could no longer be considered young, had she undulated as she served him a beer? Because he was attractive, and because we know these people who have to do with painting. But he must have dined in a good restaurant, not on the grub chez Carrel, and he wouldn't have ended his evening with the three-franc girls on *rue des Récollettes* whence Rachel, who long ago had received an ear as a Christmas present, had disappeared, carried away by syphilis or an old age that takes them early, or perhaps by some man of independent means, if the ear had brought her luck; no, that wasn't his sort of thing; besides, in Paris he had a woman who was much prettier, perhaps several. But he looked at the paintings the way Vincent had, this capitalist; Roulin thought that they were two of a kind, those two: and he could see them leaving the yellow house after a heated conversation about this or that chrome yellow, one elegant and one a little mad, one top hat, one straw, still speaking animatedly while on the threshold, leaving *sur le motif* to see who was right. He must be a painter as well, he hadn't said exactly. A painter, once again. All of this rejuvenated the postman, put a spring back into his step without any help from the absinthe. He took this youthfulness out for a stroll around the port, looking out to sea, old bearded Poseidon *coiffé d'azure,* behatted in blue, as Roulin was topped with the Prussian strain, but rather than calling it "Poseidon," Roulin named it after the cargo ships of *la Compagnie mixte,* entering with sails unfurled, Roulin using the more precise names of the anchored vessels themselves, names of dead generals and young girls that he could read off their hulls; or the names of Pacific isles where Monsieur Paul might be, Monsieur Paul who wasn't, as he had long thought, a *casseur d'assiettes* with bad table manners, but instead, a great painter whose companionship had been to his credit. By these thoughts, the sea too was rejuvenated, overflowed with dignity. To this same port, eight or ten days later, the Parisian returned at the end of a morning, stopping car and driver, his trunk filled with *Sainte-Victoires,* and not unlike a topman, in excellent spirits, headed up *rue Trigance.*

There was the same air of ceremony and amusement around this ever amiable young man. He had brought something for Mother Roulin, no doubt a bouquet, less celestial than Vincent's dahlias and less venomous than his sunflowers, soft like his irises, therefore irises that Augustine arranged right away; and for Roulin, a sealed bottle. Once again they spoke of Vincent's life, but they had already gone that route, there wasn't much left to say. The young man grew silent; he caressed the silk of his top hat before him and became absorbed in its impeccable splendor. He lifted his head and very gently, but without any amusement, he asked that the Roulins sell him their painting. The price he proposed seemed miraculous to them, many months of salary from the post office. It must have been noon; the sun was flowing onto *la Vieille Charité* across the way as if onto the flank of a pyramid; the myna bird was in rare form, whistling bits of the *Marseillaise.* This wasn't a painter, he was a merchant; Roulin wouldn't have been able to say whether he was disappointed or not; he thought about a field he had coveted long ago in Arles; he thought about ferocious revenges, about what the world owed him, a world that had pushed him into the white pit of absinthe and had endlessly watched him wallow there; he saw van Gogh leaving the yellow house in a top hat, he too, signaling imperiously to his driver, imperiously racing away; he also had the agreeable idea of officials inaugurating a bronze bust of Vincent, by *place Lamartine* or at *pont Langlois,* and he, Roulin—in the first row with all of the officials—it was he who removed the draped cloth and exhumed the little bronze beneath the Arles sky. He looked at Augustine, he said that it was difficult, that it was a remembrance and that it wouldn't be right to sell; he would have to think about it. This time, the young man stayed for lunch. In front of the uncorked bottle, the postman tried to understand why Vincent was a great painter, and the other explained as well as he could what he himself did not understand, what no one understands, and therefore Roulin, who ordinarily would have had strong opinions to express, wasn't able to get any further. The dandy talked about his profession, about Americans who know what beauty is and by their dollars are able to prove it, paintings by Vincent and Gauguin that already were climbing skyward in Manhattan's towers, higher and holier than *Notre-Dame de la Garde;* so as it turned out, that was the real end of the line for the tubes they had put on *la petite vitesse* in Arles in '88; for once in his life, maybe Roulin was amused that the capitalists had been so unscrupulous. And once again, the Parisian caressed little Marcelle's head, gripped Roulin's shoulder as he left saying that he would come back later, after they had had time to think—amiable, straightforward, juvenile—and through the window Roulin watched him descend *rue Trigance* in the heat of the day, wearing the mimosa jacket and the bright pants, an outfit well suited to a *déjeuner sur l'herbe,* but what Roulin saw for the longest time between the oyster girls' scarves, the sailors' pompons, their *bousingots,* what he saw shimmering majestically all the way to the end was the stovepipe hat, the black miter that takes the pure light, buckles it, stores it, steep as the Manhattan skyline.

The old man reflected.

He tried to imagine what Vincent would have said. He remembered, perhaps word for word, from what he had written to Théo in February of '88, having just seen Vincent for the last time and not having known it: "When I left him, I told him I will still come to see him, and he told me that we would see each other up above and through his mannerisms I understood that he was saying a prayer." Roulin, who wasn't in the habit of praying, thought that perhaps in this prayer the other was asking that he see once again the Zundert of his birth; that Théo be alerted in time to pay for the coffin; that his work not be completely forgotten, debacle that it was, and that later on, at least some young painter, exalted and unfortunate, would admire him as he had admired Monticelli, for after all, he was no Rembrandt; yet he dared to demand, perhaps, that a miracle be performed up above, and that in the eyes of a few he might pass for Rembrandt. He asked that his paintings be seen by those who would know how to look at them. But of course he didn't ask God that Roulin's portrait, given to Roulin, stay forever in the Roulins' kitchen.

He took into account all the money he had been offered. He had a little garden, the children were grown; as for the hooch, getting loaded takes less time than it used to and always comes at a fixed price, his salary sufficed. And what could you buy? Everything, once you had learned how; but that wasn't the case with him. He saw a big house along the bank of the Belsunce, or in the Meilhan lanes, behind the plane trees ventilated by the night; but how to furnish it with just the buffet, the myna bird, and his body that was heavy but not particularly important, and what do you tell the neighbors, the ship owners, the prefects? He thought about pretty girls who were more expensive and prodigious than the oyster girls, girls one doesn't buy for three francs and a blow, but with louis d'or and dollars and bundles of words he didn't know, the great white beasts almost like the oyster girls that you use the same way, that you strip and touch, whose loins you hold just the same, inside of whom you have the same great shudder, and who, just the same, get dressed and leave: Vincent would have been so happy to have them, he who went without eating for *rue des Recollettes*. Théo paid for that as well, not just for the tubes of yellow and the supposed bare minimum to live on, and it was fair that Théo foot the bill. But it was too late, Roulin could no longer replace Vincent in such an endeavor, he was too old now. What else could one really buy? Trinkets, a convertible, a cargo boat? But what would you do with it unless, in place of your own, you had a white hat, and you knew about navigation? You could go up to Paris; into Tunisia as well, even though Armand said that it's the filthiest little province in the universe. You can't buy youth in Lambesc under the Empire; or a rejuvenated Augustine; you can't buy *la Sociale*. And even if you could, what would you do with it, now?

He thought about this Parisian, who was a good boy after all, who was only half fleecing him when he could have taken him whole. This man didn't owe Roulin anything. And perhaps it was Roulin who owed him something; without him, Roulin could have died with the belief that he had been seeing things a long time ago in Arles, that what he had seen in the melon fields, for all its formidable violence, had been nothing out of the ordinary, wasn't some fabulous suffering that deserved to be rewarded no matter what the outcome, and was no longer the incarnation of who-knows-what powerful will that makes princes out of men; he could have died believing that he had seen the gesticulations of a crackpot with sunstroke, something as exaggerated and ridiculous as the trumpets from *Aïda* suddenly resonating from a brass band on a lawn where the retired come to play. To this young man he owed having known a great painter, having seen and touched something that was in many ways invisible, not just a miserable soul to whom one gives preserves. And this young man who had learned to make good use of money, as one could see from his jacket, his gestures, his kindness, would be better able to benefit from this painting of theirs; it would be of more profit to him. Sure he was a bit of a crook, but they all are: and Roulin, after he had reflected as I have said, and as any man could have perceived after a few illuminations, true or false, Roulin suddenly realized that the other only stole from the very rich who anyway had the means; from those superlative citizens who become enamored of that which they are told they should be enamored, whom we call *les amateurs;* and of course, that he was even giving them a kind of pleasure, however perverse—having convinced them that Vincent's runes were only understandable to them—he bestowed these things upon them against their weight, in gold; and when they brought their fat weights back to their homes from the steel mills, sitting in front of the wall where an imperial, untouchable Marie Ginoux rushed forward, a zouave wearing an imperial red culotte, imperial wheat at the outskirts of Arles—they took great pleasure in possessing these things, these things that escaped them even in their homes, filling them with suffering and a great suppressed rage. And this crookedness amused the republican prince in Roulin. But he was just an old, radical postman: it could be that he hadn't thought that far; perhaps he had just admitted that he really liked this little capitalist, because, of course, the dollars—the businesses that starve the poor world—he was against all that, but when it's all incarnated before you in the form of a charming man who does you no real harm, it's not that easy: even for dollars he was becoming tolerant and unconvinced. He asked for forgiveness from Blanqui's fading portrait. He looked at the tricolor atop *la Vieille Charité* and perhaps he no longer saw within its folds, as he usually did, a flag of one color charged with putting an end to evil, billowing over our paradise with the help of the beast representing History, as Tarascon is represented by *la tarasque,* the dragon that pestered her until a saint drove it away, Tarascon where *la tarasque* waits no longer, the patient beast, blind and fossorial, impotent, the old crone in Marx's coat of arms.

So the young man returned one last time and dined. At the end of the meal, the postman took on a serious air, as wily as a muzhik about to drive off with his boyar, and said that they were to talk business; there was a silence; the young man was smiling slightly; Roulin began; he was giving the painting, on the condition, however, that people knew that it had been given, by the artist himself, to Monsieur Joseph-Etienne Roulin, something which, for example, could be engraved on the edge of the frame; and he was giving the frame as well; this he added while laughing, but he worried that it might be refused, just as he hoped that this gift be reported in the Arles *Forum républicain*—and why not in a Parisian paper?—since van Gogh was famous now and since the young man had some connections: he wanted to boast a little. I believe in little else but the bright joy that illuminated the dandy's eye; Roulin had seen something dance there not unlike Fouquier's look at having taken a head, and suddenly in the top hat he saw Fouquier's great cocked hat, black as well, but plumed; and I'm sure that this wasn't the look the young man had, it wasn't that hat he was wearing: he was an easy-going guy, a dealer. He smiled and laughed because he was moved. Of course he stood and embraced them. They drank. To mark the moment, Roulin stood before his Saint Abbacyr, still hanging on the wall, and sang a *Marseillaise* or an old topman's tune, *Jean-François de Nantes,* his voice strong, his Asshurian beard, plastered down when singing the low notes, his eye peering far past *Notre-Dame de la Garde* and the blue line of the Vosges toward the paradise of the Beaux Arts; the myna bird was thrilled by all of this. When very late the young man tipsily descended the stairs and left down *rue Trigance* with his painting under his arm; when with his head lifted toward the stars he ran joyously in the deserted night, the air whistling in his ears, he thought he heard next to him, above him, above the colossal and hollow mass of *la Vieille Charité,* in every way lost deep in the black, an enormous flight of swallows frolicking and filling the night.

ROULIN DIED IN SEPTEMBER 1903, the date to which the scholarly books attest, before Augustine, before Armand and the others, as one would expect. Perhaps he died in the hospital and the very same room in which Rimbaud had died a decade earlier, since we're romantics; from cirrhosis; from pulmonary afflictions caused by tobacco; from a stroke after a fit of rage, a hangover, or a mild vexation. It would seem too fitting that upon returning too early one evening after having gotten too much sun in his little garden in the low-grown countryside, he had fallen toward Estaque, in a little road that snakes its way above the great gulf, a yew tree at its end, a cypress. So he has fallen there and he knows all too well what's happening to him, he's not even thinking; it's the *Grand Soir* when he is to die. The sea shimmers; the god topped with azure looks on without blinking: he's an old captain; from the earth come crows, and seagulls from the sea. There's gravel in Roulin's beard; he tries to grab his hat; it has fallen a little farther; he can't do it; the leeks, he can't keep hold of them either, he lets them go: and all of a sudden he is dead, immediately elsewhere he drives his boyar through fields of dahlias; as they pass close by, you hear the little bells jingling. Beyond all constraints the unconstrained prince leaps into the blue. Maybe he's beautiful, but we can't see him.

Who can say what is beautiful and as a result, amongst men, is deemed worthless or worthwhile? Is it our eyes, which are the same, Vincent's, the postman's, and my own? Is it our hearts, which a trifle can seduce, which a trifle can dismiss? Is it you, young man sitting with your hat placed next to you chez Ambroise Vollard, talking animatedly about painting with beautiful women? Or you, paintings roosting in Manhattan, merchandise whose enlightened fads nourish the dollars, doubtlessly drawing them nearer to God as well? Is it you, Browning? Perhaps it's you, Old Captain topped in blue, looking at a little heap of Prussian blue fallen on a road; it's you, white beasts, learned and mute, whose very volumes we caress far from here on *rue des Récollettes,* who know exactly what three francs is worth; it's you, crows flying up above that no one can buy, no one can command, which do not speak and are only eaten during the worst famines, whose feathers even Fouquier wouldn't want in his hat, dear crows to whom the Lord gave wings of matte black, a cry that cracks, the flight of a stone, and from the mouth of His servant Linneaus came the imperial name *Corvus corax.* It's you, roads. Trees that die like men. And you, sun.

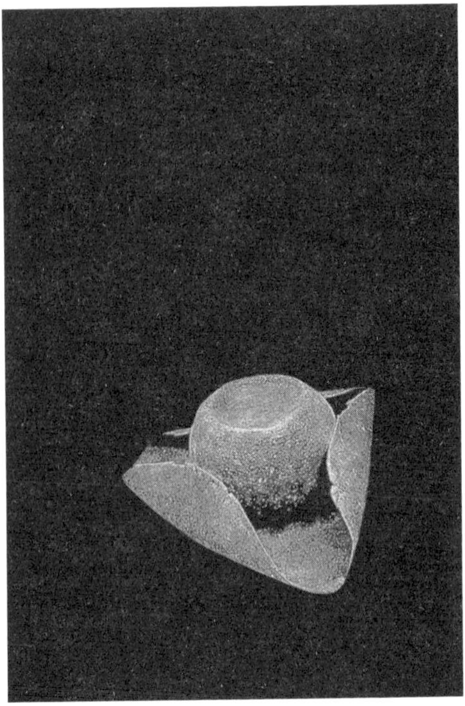

God Is Never Through

We knew Francisco Goya. Our mothers, or perhaps our grandmothers, saw him arrive in Madrid. They saw him knocking on doors, on all the doors, stooped, benignly; they saw him not be named to the academies, saw him praise those who were, saw him return docilely to his province to paint more of his stiff brand of schoolboy mythologies, and once again saw him present them to our court painters, one year, two years later; only to fail once again, to clear out again, taking a poorly rendered Venus or Moses with him, painted in the open country and brought to town on the back of an ass: all this at seventeen, at twenty, at twenty-seven years old. Our mothers saw him and they remember him little, or not at all. But it's not possible that they didn't cross paths with him one day—opening a door, for example, in one of the academies, in a palace where they had a crush on some painter of renown whom they were going to meet, Mengs, Giaquinto, Gasparini, or one of the Tiepolos, or some other who wasn't one of those but who took himself to be the best of them, a handsome, fastidious little Italian with gray hair and a sweeping touch, with that accent that makes your heart flip-flop, a man in love with women and loved by them, a man busy poking holes in ceilings and filling them with blonde angels falling through endless skies, Italian clouds, trumpets—it isn't possible that while pushing a door with a fluttering heart, a hand primping hair, fluffing a dress, that they hadn't found the fat little man from Saragossa behind them—frozen, little more than a statue with sketches under its arm, chubby, stunned, struggling to smile; it isn't possible that for an instant they hadn't cast a questioning, perhaps annoyed, glance on this dolt; and so he stepped out of their way a bit too hastily, bowed a bit too low, seemed to want more than anything to disappear and even so remained there revolving around the condesa and the Italian like some fly that won't stop buzzing around one's head, like some dog that's always getting kicked, saying nothing and rolling his bulging eyes, unable to avert them from the fringe of her skirt, where, occasionally, a petticoat might show, or an ankle, and when the maestro at last deigned to look upon a Moses of Aragon or a Venus of the Paseo unrolled before them, perhaps praising them out of good taste, out of politesse, or just to get rid of him, he would stoop further still, appearing ready to collapse into tears and shuffling backward toward the door, bow after bow; and before leaving he didn't forget to look up again at this infinitely blue ceiling, like some peasant marveling at elephants on a fairground, a peasant who remained wily all the same, even incredulous, irritating, such that if the fat lips on the brink of tears said "What a marvel, Master. A Raphael, a Raphael, really," then all the while the bulging eyes would be sizing up the woman beneath her dress, calculating the cost of the Italian's boots and cuffs, while still passionately venerating the sweeping touch, the talent apparent in such skies, in such Holy Trinities, in the mythological knowledge and the painter's seductive appeal to ladies, to academies, to ceilings: because with so much hope and so few natural gifts the little dolt from Saragossa couldn't hope, he couldn't hate, he could only sit himself down and wait for his time to come, uncertain whether it would come, patient, awkward, and panicked, all in equal measure. They saw that he was afraid like so many others they had forgotten, and we too would have forgotten him had fear been his only attribute. It could also have been that during a stroll sometime one May when the mornings are still beautiful, at *la Florida* or along the Prado, our mothers or grandmothers had half noticed the dumpy silhouette during one of their strolls, saw him sidle up in his cape, a vestige of winter amidst gladiola, frowning, peering somberly out from the shade of the green oaks at those who were riding in carriages in the sun and were dressed *à la Française,* women in all their finery, all those most bubbly and best named, and when don Rafael Mengs or Signor Giambattista Tiepolo arrived in their gilded carriages, our mothers and grandmothers then saw the little cape make a mad rush forward, exiting the shadows and appearing in the light, an owl suddenly flushed out with sombrero to his breast, in a bow, his reverent glance fixed high above on the invisible halo of the Master piercing the great ceiling of Madrid's sky, his trembling face and smile monument to this apparition, panicked, and perhaps miserable. And the master waved to this fat young man who wanted to do well by himself. But it could also be that our mothers had seen something different; that they hadn't been shocked by all the fawning, the clumsiness, the trembling lips that are features shared by all those who arrive from the provinces with their ignorance, their appetites; that suddenly our mothers noticed how he wore his cape: because when the sombrero was off and his gaze had become deferential before Señor Mengs, whose words overflowed with tired old talk of the Greeks that the little Saragossan lapped up—along with monologues on eternal Beauty according to Winckelmann, on the human face's tangential relationship to those of the gods, on all the legendary *pittura,* all the Prussian theories—it could have been that our mothers and grandmothers, who didn't know a whit about the fads of such serious men, had watched that chubby face over there—concentrating, desperately trying to understand it all as if panic stricken—suddenly come undone and sparkle with a maddening desire to laugh; and it may be that, taken aback, our mothers had paid close attention to this, this blasphemy or this insolent force that Mengs, completely wrapped up in himself, didn't begin to notice: though the little Aragonese was sincerely, dolorously trying to understand, he didn't believe a word of it. Our mothers must have momentarily paused to ask themselves why this little man had chosen to paint, if painting were seemingly both punishment and prank, pushing him to the brink of tears and then contorting him with laughter; perhaps not just to get his foot in the door, but to ensure that it was well shod; perhaps also to suffer and to get to make fun of everything, since mankind is curious. They observed all of this, the madness of a man who wasn't mad: and he wasn't clumsy at all, taking leave of the master and the beauty on the street by way of bows only made awkward by the paintings he had under his arms, stammering "Leonardo, Maestro, yes, the angels, the smile, the space," taking great care to pack up his Moses on the packsaddle of his ass, and heading off astride him, leaning over the big ears, stroking his beast to whom he perhaps spoke of Raphael; our mothers and grandmothers wondered if what they heard when the man and the ass reached the end of the road was the ass's braying or the man's laughter; but perhaps each one, under the burden of bad paintings and too many allusions, was crying in his own way. He closed the door on himself once again, he plunged back into the Floridian greenery, cropping his ass. He went back to Aragon. He may as well not even have existed.

What did he do in Aragon? He painted, Señora, of course. And there, our mothers did not see him, but his own mother did, doña Gracia, and the daughters of those whom he took to bed, washerwomen from Ebre or whores; we don't know anything about them because they generally don't say anything while beating laundry and rolling onto their backs, tending their chilblain and their native shame, obstinate, lips pursed, arrogant, and ruined; but perhaps in an unknown album he drew them, on a gold background, just as he saw them and without question exactly as they were, incomplete, their faces somewhat disturbed, like the face of a river sullied by blue washing powder, their gazes like a pond, and all of their features hesitating between a childhood barely tasted and on the brink of collapse, and eternal old age. No, it is very unlikely that he painted them that way; it's even unlikely that he'd had them, because he set joy aside for later, for when he would be Mengs or Tiepolo, when condesas are yours for the taking and ceilings are there for you to paint; and his mother told our mothers that he had been a good and proper son, not undisciplined but industrious, swinging open the door to his father's studio before dawn, his father the master gilder who had been a good and proper husband, thus crossing this studio where his candle illuminated reredoses peopled with paradise and devotional statues of San Isidro, San Antonio, Santiago, all of them staring out at you, blessing you, all of them golden and in perfect relief, bright and true like all that the Señor created. So, said doña Gracia, at dawn he would enter his father's studio of shrines and crosses, passing through it to reach his very own, much smaller studio that had been granted in a corner of his father's—because the son could no longer work with Luzán, his master, they had had a falling out; and all day long he wore himself out painting, maybe Venuses and prophets, certainly some San Isidros and some Santiagos too, as fair as el Señor had made them and clearly calling to Him; and when doña Gracia came in with sausage, with chocolate, she found him on his knees in front of his painting, his nose to the canvas, with little strokes ironing out one of those impeccable frocks in which Zurbarán decked out his chartreuse saints, or one of those magical starched cowls that either pious housewives or angels must just have ironed; or yet again, but more sullen this time, as if he had just crushed some reds into the wounds of the Savior, agonizing over the holy hands in the Italian manner, those delicate fingers, happy, visible, in which every knuckle is delineated, bending and caressing the miraculous space, thick and bright; other times he stood as tall as his little body would, with the air of one painting vast backgrounds, insolent but precise, with all the brio of the Venetians: he was playing, said doña Gracia, he was like a child on his father's shoulders. She didn't say, doña Gracia, that while the father was gilding a beard or Saint Peter's sacred keys with his little brush, he might hear a curse from the other side of the studio, a canvas bursting like a drum, and the little fatso laughing cruelly while hacking his stretcher to bits; that sort of thing mothers pretend not to know about. On the other hand, what she said that we do want to believe is that he liked to horse around on public holidays, in their little patch of land in the countryside of Fuendetodos, to thrash around with the feverish athleticism that seems to take particular possession of fat men; in the company of the little toughs his age he pestered some baby bull and sometimes even a grown one, some thoroughly real, thoroughly black beast, although this was probably in an impromptu arena with an impromptu cape, some red rag still dripping with dye; but with a real sword too, made of iron that cuts. Even in a place as lost as Fuendetodos there would have been bulls to slay. This we all know, because later he prided himself on it, as though he had passed his insouciant jeunesse at such play, fighting bulls with only cape, dress culottes, and pink stockings, not fiddling desperately with Italian draperies and Sevillian frocks in a studio jammed with vermilion saints destined for use in the sundry chapters; and he talked as though the spectacle had always taken place in the light of day, in the light of the July of his youth, a youth invented for the benefit of others and perhaps even for himself. But we, we didn't see him fighting bulls; and nothing prevents us from thinking that beneath the confusion of a rainy March sky of his twentieth year, he thought he witnessed a perfect disaster, perfectly in keeping with our botched Creation: it rained that day on Fuendetodos, on the smoking black fur, the soft nostrils; slipshod hooves lost their footing, mud splattered everywhere; something suffered there, as likely the sky and its rain as the beast and its matador; the matador wiped his eyelids with his forearm to see the beast clearly so he could stab it with his rapier; no sun burst forth at the final blow, *la mise à mort,* no flurry of blows, only something that dripped a little, like a bad painting one would happily destroy. And around this heap of ruined black meat that one would happily destroy, heavy and formless, with blue cheeks, conceived during one of those rapid, furious couplings in the fields, the Aragonese peasantry shouted lifeless curses into the rain, dancing a jig as old as time, all gray but for scarlet on one of their shoulders, the cape which already was fading. One doesn't fight bulls in the rain, Señora? Ah, of course. The impeccable chests of white horses rise up through the blue of the ceilings. Winged creatures leave their weights to the land and carry their shapes and songs above, into the eternally clement heavens. Yes, said doña Gracia, he fought bulls on public holidays, but during the week he took great care to paint pretty paintings. He was industrious.

And of course he toiled away dutifully; because without such industry, he wouldn't have landed the little commissions that we know he honored in Sobadriel, in Remolinos, in Aula Dei, and with the Carthusians, little towns just a stone's throw from Saragossa, less than a morning away by donkey from the studio filled with golden saints, and there in the monasteries, in the little palaces of parvenus, in forgotten, tumble-down churches, other portraits of saints were waiting for him, this time his own portraits, though scarcely less golden; saints whose commissioners were looking for an easygoing dauber who was unpretentious, not Italian in his ways but who painted in the Italian manner, who preferred the soul to the shape, as one says in the provinces, in short someone suitable, someone deferential to his assistants and, toward the churchwarden, polite. What more particular merit won him his commissions? Please Señora, no, not his talent, which perhaps a few clairvoyants had perceived when the rest of the world had its eyes closed; not the royal palette that he did not yet have, nor the great spirit that perhaps he never had; not the gift of divine and eccentric observation that the ignorant ascribe to artists: come now, even we have eyes. No particular merit, then, but his willingness, the way he understood that by rejecting his project one year someone was accepting it the next, the overzealousness apparent in coming from Saragossa on his own ass rather than on one of the abbey's, and the speed with which he animated a face, altering it with minute and disastrous additions that a prior—keen on antiques, who long ago had made the trip to Saint Peter's and therefore had seen it all—suggested paternally, and not without feeling. He was in hell, really: not because he didn't know how to paint, because he had learned all that, something half mankind can learn, indeed, anyone, with practice; but because a real interest in painting—a field in which, who knows why, he had been tossed like a bull into an arena or each man into his own life—had eluded him; but nonetheless he loved painting, as every man loves his own life, and perhaps as even a bull loves his arena; there are those who have said that what exasperated him in those days was having to throw a tribe of angels onto a wall or toss up a meeting between the Living God and his humble little Witnesses, and they note how well he painted those humble folk, and go on to talk our ears off about how he loved only the humble. And we all know that it exasperated him equally to have to toss some muddy washerwomen and some local crazies into a little album, later on: we all know that painting, what he called painting, was always unattainable for him, and that was why he painted. Well, not exactly: it brought money, too, had fattened the priceless Mengs and the more reasonable but equally unreasonable Giaquinto, and he wanted to fatten up, he too, the little fatso. So, in order to fatten himself up, you understand, in the little Carthusian monasteries in the countryside, he put a little Tiepolo into the blue skies, a little Zurbarán into draperies that fall to Earth and break; he made clouds upon which to sit when one is Up Above, and victorious wings clinging to angelic shoulder blades like Mardi Gras masks; a general indifference prevails in the humble little witness, the saints martyred and mitered, drawn and quartered or painted in purple, as if none of them is there at all. He fiddled with things to make them look pretty, not that he even knew the meaning of such a word, Señora, what we mean when we call something *pretty.* He exaggerated everything, even modesty, because he thought that a day would arrive when he would do as Mengs or Tiepolo had, that is, would pocket what they had pocketed; but without question, most of the time, his exaggerations took the form of absolute fury, invisibly, or of absolute laughter, the sound of which we are perhaps wiser to ignore; and if that poor old woman who polishes the gold of the altar and changes the spoiled lilies in the vases had entered the chapel and heard this laugh, and, though forbidden to, had lifted her head to look at the frescoist, holding onto his scaffold with two hands, beneath another gaggle of archangels, she really would have had to ask why he was laughing. "Oh," Francisco would have said, "that old half-blind sick-dog-of-a-prior stared a little too long at my Saint Jerome and just took off with his tail between his legs, as if the saint had walked out of the woods and bitten him." And at this the poor woman would have laughed too.

This for ten years. His hour came, that little hour when he

said to himself, at around thirty years of age: Well then, maybe I'll be Mengs, with God's help. God helped him in the unexpected form of a man whom you do not remember, Señora, but who long ago had been a painter, very much of the court, and who would have been more so had he not wasted his time being jealous of his shadow; a man who, upon meeting the little fatso, found him inoffensive, took an interest in him and decided to push him before the world, as a foil and as a valet; yes, God put someone in Goya's path who was more smug than Tiepolo the Younger, more silver-tongued than a Neapolitan, and more useless than Mengs—the great Francisco Bayeu.

ABOUT THAT, THIS LITTLE TOSS of loaded dice, we know everything that one can know, because poor Josefa told us about it, or she kept so quiet about it that she said just as much, Josefa Goya, *née* Bayeu; Josefa with her meagre little braid rolled into a bun at the nape of her neck, her hair that was neither exactly blonde nor precisely red, and her other ambivalent features, her weak smile and her kind eyes; Josefa who gave him forty years of her life until death, her own, and to whom were given the alms of a single small portrait of her, one in forty years—this portrait, which she kept devoutly, which I saw in her room, and before which she was sitting with her hands clasped in front of her and with the same timid smile that the portrait captured, clasped hands and timid smile, perhaps thanking God for this miracle, or excusing herself for her immodesty: he had painted her once, with the same colors and the same hand, he who painted the queen and the cardinal dukes, infants and their toys; Josefa whom he called Pepa and who was as necessary to him as the big brush from Lyon and the smoky black that filled backgrounds and that one didn't notice but that were the painting, were space, without which the richly brocaded princes of the foreground might as well disappear into nothingness; Pepa whom perhaps he loved, as she didn't dare say and didn't dare think, whom he knocked up ten times for nothing, except that one time when little Javier was born, Javier who wasn't to rush double-time to join his brothers and sisters in the grave, lifeless despite their perfect forms, completed like some painting, who ended up rotting away like their father's paintings; mother of all these little cadavers and of Javier's living body, Javier who was smug and who was doted on by his father, who had his own son Mariano—who was even more smug, if that's possible, and was adored by his grandfather; Josefa, the despised sister of Francisco Bayeu, who passed into the hands of a Francisco Goya who really wanted her, in the middle of July, in the middle of Madrid, or almost—in the little church of Santa María in a Madrid suburb.

She did not say that she was happy, Pepa, on this 25th of July. But telling of it twenty-five years later still made her blush, not as you blush, Señora, but the way unassuming blondes are wont to, self-effacing themselves to featurelessness, confused by their pleasure and its manifestation, then losing that pleasure for others having seen it, such that the recollection of their joy is so insignificant, since this great, departed emotion prompts no envy from others, is barely of interest, is but a simulacrum of comprehension, is pity; they're used to it, these self-effacing blondes, they talk about it. So she told us how happy he had been, him, her Francisco, this 25th of July, wearing his pearl gray morning coat *à la française* that was a little tight on him, certainly too small, but that made him look taller, and not as fat as they said, but chubby cheeked, yes, like a child, and like a child enjoying everything, getting married, seeing a magpie fly over Santa María when the bells began to ring, the little children of honor all in red who were getting tangled up in their bouquets of white gladiola, in their little approximations of the motions of men, and these round eyes they suddenly have, these tears they spill who knows why—because a cloud passed over the sun, because the step to the square is too high to reach, because the world doesn't stop at the instant of their joy. He was like them, Pepa said. And if he was delighted, it wasn't because he was joining the Bayeu clan, as spiteful gossips call it, by some mix of calculation and barbarism; it wasn't because he was now nearly in Madrid, at its very gates; it wasn't because he suddenly became—as if by the touch of a magic wand, by the taking of a poor girl's virginity— the brother-in-law of Francisco Bayeu, the king's painter, Mengs's favorite disciple and his assured dauphin, sharp tongued and omnipresent, incapable, strong; and it wasn't because on the same occasion, in the same bag, he became brother-in-law to Ramón and Manuel Bayeu, no less painters and no less incapable, but milder, with duller features and duller wills, long since stuck in the gloomy palette of Bayeu-le-Grand, foils both of them and errand boys, of a certain sort; "No," said Pepa, "this is all just malicious gossip: he was happy to enter into my brother's family, that is true, but it was because he liked him, my brother, whom he admired and listened to talk about painting—he knew everything, my brother—and my fiancé still had a few things to learn. He was, perhaps, also happy to marry me, but that, I don't know."

Just look: they're leaving Santa María, on this beautiful

July morning in Madrid, when the heat is already building, but is still young. Their tricornes are in their hands; Bayeu is wearing a deep brown morning coat and ochre yellow breeches, he is just behind Goya and, since he's taller, he puts a hand on Goya's shoulder and gestures at the fine weather. The two look up, and all of this charms them as much as it does us: painters surround them and even some counts, the embroidered vests of *majos,* great blue sashes spanning ducal chests *à la française,* liveries more manifest than their coats of arms, a thousand dresses, this one *à la française,* that one in *maja;* and up above, bells are leaping, delicate monsters of heavy bronze that are to the ear what flowers are to the eyes, and just like flowers they turn their heads modestly but unfailingly to greet the great, immodest dome of the sky; fans and tricornes too are flowers, says Bayeu, leaning on Goya's shoulder. But what's this? Is the groom frowning, and what is the bride about to shout? What's happening suddenly, Señora, above these nuptials? A shower? In the middle of July, when the skies were just so clear? It can't be that God is angry, as they say; he doesn't bother with us any more, he wouldn't show his face now. And it can't be the Inquisition swooping down with pyres and carts, sanbenitos and thunderous, chanted Latin exhortations; the Inquisition is nowhere in this storm, of course. Where is this execrable grandeur that is falling on their heads coming from? Whose poor brushwork is this? Tricornes are rising into the Boreas, and it isn't the wind that has taken them, they are climbing, blackly, toward all this black so within reach, with a flap of wings they are there, because the sky is no higher than the shortest of Santa María's spires, such strange birds flying above, and you say, now, that it's a death knell we hear? And the poor guests on the stone steps, how helpless they seem, everything falling from their hands, everyone bending to pick things up, bending, pits of shadow falling across their faces, their brutish chins, their fleshy ugliness, their beastly mouths, Señora, that twist and turn outward, deepening, displaying teeth and tongues, they are past speech, not from some ugliness of the soul, no, it's not hunger or lust—in this weather!—and not fear because they knew that the gust of wind would come: it's sorrow, Señora, it's such sorrow. The sky weighs on their shoulders like a great sack. We bear it as best we can. And what now? Who has killed this woman, bound on the steps, head dangling down? And the water running over her hiked skirts, on her unfortunate face, in her hair, neither blonde nor red, on her meagre belly from which Javier won't come, from which ten little corpses and semi-corpses won't either. Bayeu and his brothers, his friend Zapater, the dukes, the old master gilder who came jubilantly from Saragossa in his Sunday best—all these Nebuchadnezzars around her on all fours, who graze and who are painters, who graze and who are dukes, who above all certainly are crying, but how can you tell in all this rain. It must be the wind that felled them, come now, it's not madness, it's not wickedness. Is it them? Go see. They all look alike; you can't tell who's devouring whom. But the little fatso over there who's running away down the lane wearing his pearl gray morning coat, dripping wet, dripping beneath the cloudbursts like the palette of some slob, this tubby imp exulting beneath the gush from the rain gutters, it seems that we recognize him, his kindness, his *joie de vivre,* his modesty, and the big knife in his skirts. A knife, where? In any case, not in the hands of Francisco Goya who turns while smiling toward Francisco Bayeu and says:

God Is Never Through

yes, flowers, everywhere, fans and white mantillas blooming like hawthorns, toy dogs, *majos* and their ponytails and the buckles on their breeches, red bows on the Swiss tricornes, women's hands budding phalanx upon phalanx as though petal to petal, and look, brother, these little children all in red watching us with their eyes so clear, as though they're posing for us: he's exaggerating, of course, as usual, but that's a small sin. Come on, it was just a dream. A bizarre dream that came to me. Without them, life would be a bad dream. No, it's beautiful out, look closer, Señora, all is quiet in the church square, everyone is gleaming with color and joy, a perfect sky out of Tiepolo is above them, deep, far: the Creator made all this blue and he left nothing there for us to retouch. Thus we may marry in a pearl gray morning coat, we may have sons. Nothing need be repeated. And the white and the black of the magpie sitting in a tree in Santa María Square, frozen— its beak suspicious and sharp, its eyes round and clearly drawn, this white and this black are so clearly delineated by such majestic lines, white feather against black feather, in careful little strokes, never blending together, never blending into the leaves either, nor into the big blue leaves high above. Goya watches this magpie.

He holds Pepa gently by the arm.

He moves down the stairs, he hesitates and puts his tricorne back on, then takes it off again, then decides finally, yes: he sets foot upon his parcel of worldly bliss. You know what bliss is, Señora? These periods in life, quite frequent during youth, though not so frequent that one may count on them, when you have faith in yourself without having to believe you're someone other than yourself, when you hope that in a year, in ten years, you'll have made it, which is to say you'll have arrived, you'll have what you wanted, once and for all you'll be what you wanted to be, and you'll remain that way; but right now you suffer, you're a little less or a little more than yourself, but in ten years you'll be there, there where you should be: bliss is such a small thing to suffer, and we all know that during these five or six years Goya was happy. He was patient, he chided himself for his mediocrity, he applied himself to making his name; and he was a little bit sneaky on this count, a touch of talent and a touch of imposture, a talent for color, for low bows to the princes, bowing and scraping, stuffy or spirited discussions about masters, technique, finishing touches, profits: this with Bayeu who thought he was Mengs; with Mengs who was already dying but who was sticking to the belief that he was the word made paint; with young colleagues no less talented or sneaky than he, who wanted to fatten themselves as well, have their own carriages, paint well, to be Mengs or Tiepolo one day, depending on whether their tastes and their palettes drew them toward angels as stiff as popes or to those more suave and ambiguously fleshed. And of this so-called imposture: if you succeed at making clear distinctions between things, is it imposture? Why wouldn't painting be a farce, since life is one, if marrying poor Pepa and toadying to Bayeu gets you princely commissions, and the glances of duchesses? Come on, it was a pleasure destroying those stretchers long ago in Saragossa, a pleasure to die of laughter inside when Mengs was talking about the Golden Proportions. All of that was child's play; it was a betrayal of the brotherhood of painters, of painting, perhaps, and of the very working of things: imagine an augur laughing in the face of a great captain, serious and nervous, leaning over some chicken guts over which other augurs are nodding, interpretively. The great captain loses his battle, the augurs are hunted down, everyone knows that his misfortune is meaningless, who gains from any of it? No: what is meaningful, what painting means, is to toil like a galley slave on the sea, with that furor, with that helplessness: and when the work is done, when the penal colony opens for an instant, when the painting is hung, then say to everyone, to the princes who'll believe it, the people who'll believe it, the painters who won't believe it, that it came to you in one fell swoop, against your will and miraculously in harmony with it, a spring day blooming from your brushtips, that something took possession of your hand and carried it like angels draw chariots with a single finger, something like Tiepolo returned to Earth, all of *la pittura* flowing through you, all the beauty of mother nature in your grasp (can you hear, Señora, the great, silent guffaws in the heads of painters everywhere?)—that art just came to you, winged like an angel, easy as a *maja*. Why not imagine a galley slave on the bridge of his galley, a ball and chain on each foot, hands dead, swearing that the sea itself had kindly moved his oar for him, had purged him of his pain, had cradled it—and why not, since it is the source of his pain?

He played this game for five or six years, and this time blissfully, because now (or have I already told you?), he knew how to paint, and he didn't ignore that he now knew how to paint. Not that he believed in his painting, as they say; not that he then believed in Painting, in its inaccessibility, the absence and much wished for arrival of which had tortured him, long ago, this dolorous hope that had perhaps seized this child amongst gilded saints that watched over him, asked him things, this dream, more fleeting than a shadow and never seen, born of the prodigious conjunction of a hand and a little space that becomes the world; and the world would be born out of that hand. Yes, Señora, what he had wanted long ago was for the galley slave to sign the sea with his oar, and since it couldn't be that way, why not just return to his bench beside those like him and labor, perhaps happily, wait for his grub, and row. Painting was nothing more than that; and he knew how to paint, if there wasn't more to it than that. Certainly he was happy, on his bench, on the *Calle del Reloj,* Pepa fixing his grub, princes wanting a quail hunt, a picnic, a swing scene, and without much effort he painted guns and quail, grapes, a pig under some trees, with fine blues and pinks, restrained reds that nonetheless reach out to the viewer, all Giaquinto. Such tranquillity. He thought at last that he was well out of it. From class to class he peacefully rose toward death, the death of an excellent painter. And an evening awaited him where amongst Italian arbors he would sit contentedly drinking, old, a master, in the leafy shadows with one hundred ceilings behind him, don Francisco Goya.

FOR THE MOMENT, THOUGH, he still is young and disciple of everyone, is sitting beneath a Spanish arbor, near Manzanares, in May; at the *Auberge du Coq;* in 1778; with Ramón Bayeu and José del Castillo, painters; with Josefa? Please, Señora. With a bullfighter, Señora? Why not: so they brought along Pedro Romero or his brother José, or both, because in the company of these butchers, one is bound to attract *majas* like wasps to honey. So one of these *majas* they picked up told us of this gathering of men of few scruples at play with their shirts agape, of their babble that overflowed with talk of coin of the realm, and this abundance of foliage bent over these men of gain, charitable wines in greedy throats, greedy, but friendly, fleeing the pain; one of them—and perhaps it's this one actually, Narcissa is her name, I think—her thigh is being groped under the lace, under the table, in the shadows, by the little Aragonese: because, Señora, you know he loved us very much, as they say, however infrequently—pretty or not—we came under his hand; he painted us, without ceremony he touched us, under a table or on top, with words, touching us one way or another, and without ceremony consuming us—because by that time he had given himself the right to pleasure, and it was no longer washerwomen—these you could show off—and when you paint ceilings for princes and you want to enjoy yourself you have the right to, like a prince. And since all that, for the little fatso, was no more trouble than the right words said at the right moment and the numerous skirts hiked at the right moment, I won't say too much about it, if you don't mind. There was no harm in it, his sin didn't lie there. Therefore, she, *la maja,* said that our three painters feasted extravagantly with their matador, their foil, this living proof, who was a little tiresome, a little simple, but so profitable, proof on display that they weren't just priggish pedants, that they preferred life to painting, blood to pigment: and if they got together to enjoy flowers and wine, May and young girls, it wasn't to celebrate a living painter or to morn one dead; it was, my sweet, because they had landed—because Bayeu-le-Grand had landed for them—a fabulous commission, a fat commission for the lean newcomers.

King and Court were in Aranjuez, as they were every spring, with the flowing waters and the fields of jonquils; and from amongst the jonquils the king somehow got it into his head that he missed his great collection of Spanish paintings, left at the Pardo, and in the Pardo itself, on the walls of this immense gallery in which he was accustomed to dressing himself right out of bed, as kings do, a hundred steps and as many dignitaries between shoe and morning coat, another hundred steps between morning coat and sash, fifty hidalgos between sash and glove, and upon leaving the bedroom still rubbing his eyes he'd see the tricorne on the far wall, so small against the blue velvet, like a shepherd's coat spied by the Asturias at the end of a pass, this last little piece of black that he would don only at the end of one Velázquez's perilous, mute parades or of Ribera's black ones, dignitaries with panaches, real or painted, ancestors dead and alive; the live ones followed him everywhere, to Aranjuez in May, to Granja in August, to Escurial in Autumn; but the dead ones who remained in the Pardo, unruffled on their steep walls, these he missed; perhaps he needed this mountain of dead men to welcome him to the breaking day, men who, once kings in flesh, now live only in their dreams: and through the chain of five or six living dignitaries he made it known to Bayeu-le-Grand that he wanted to see appear on his little levee, at Granja, at Aranjuez, all the dead dignitaries and forbears, that he wanted a little reflection of this great mountain he had in his mind, wherever he dressed; and Bayeu-le-Grand had charged Bayeu-le-Petit, del Castillo, and Goya, who weren't dignitaries but who were quick with their hands, to reproduce over again these reproductions of dead men, in engravings, and at a good wage.

And this wage that they hadn't yet pocketed—the *maja* told us—they were already well into it that day at the *Auberge du Coq*. The afternoon is waning, the sun is changing, and now the tricornes are fully in the sun, are resting on the tablecloth, are absorbing all this light without a wrinkle, as black as they were before, when the green arbor shaded them at midday. More wine arrives. They're ripe, our brigands. Until then they had been talking about reales, ducats, about brushing elbows with princes, about all the babies' hands they'll kiss and the big sashes they'll fasten; there was a small dispute when they had divvied up their booty: Ramón is Bayeu's brother, del Castillo is the oldest; whereas Francisco, what has he done other than his cartoons—very beautiful, certainly—for the tapestry weavers of Santa Barbara? So his share will be a quarter, still a nice piece of change, right Francisco? He held me tighter, said the girl, and higher up, and by God I let him, the wine, all the sun on the table, the green leaves. His other hand was crumpling the tablecloth. He groused a little. And they let him, promising him a bit more and then he relented, probably the wine, or friendship, and Roberto's big arm around the shoulders of the angry little guy: Oh come on Francisco, the King's chamber! Now—but all of this is growing hazy, says the *maja,* I can barely hear them—it's not nickels and dimes they're talking about, not reales, it's another sonorous species they speak of now, weighty names buzzing around with the weighty wasps and all the wine in our heads, they're brawling over the big names, they're dividing up the work, our thieves, you get Murillo, you get Velázquez, *I take Ribera,* says del Castillo. At the next table, cattlemen are having at each other too, over cows. Goya is in the midst of shooing a wasp with his hand, the other hand, when they suggest he take Velázquez: that's fine, him or someone else, he's not too into the conversation since they promised him 2,500 in cash, his hand has been busy with me, he looks above us at the inn's sign, a great rooster of white iron, wings spread, and so I look up at it too, no longer in control of myself; you might say that it's singing, like when someone had disowned I can't remember whom; Francisco leans toward me, tells me, squinting, that with some dove feathers and some pink roses we'd have an angel presiding over a *paradiso:* he described it all, cattlemen, drunk painters, wasps fallen in wine, trees of paradise, and me with him, at his side. He laughs, his head in his arms on the table, amongst impeccable black hats and the carafes. He's had a lot to drink. I turned my head, no one was looking at me. The tricornes aren't moving, night is coming; there is no more wine in our glasses; I smooth my dress. He lifts his head, he laughs until he is crying, he says: *Oh sure, Velázquez.* Poor Francisco.

Off they went to the Pardo, the next day or a week later. You can imagine them, Señora, just as I see them, entering the great gate, early one morning in May. They're on horseback, Goya is lagging behind, he doesn't ride well, he'd be happier on foot, but they have horses just the same, gaudy ones, isabels or piebalds, as different as you can get from the donkey that took you to the Carthusian monasteries lost beneath their bells on the fringes of forests, and that you preferred to the piebald, but now on which you wouldn't want to be seen. The morning coat is *à la française,* the vest quilted, the gloves butternut yellow, and this handsome, fresh green redingote that befits spring: he's gotten decked out to see the king, even if the king isn't there; at least that's what he thinks. So he rode through the gates. What beautiful weather. Bells are rising, he feels as light. There are Flemish guards everywhere, grooms, turnkeys, stewards; you don't salute them, one after another the doors open marvelously before your steps, one after another; you toss the reins of your horse to some bit player, you don't look at these nameless faces since you are who you are, Francisco Goya, who in ten years will be Tiepolo and who already is climbing this staircase where the king walks every day of every winter. At last inside the square, the final guard bows deeply because this one, he's a prince—what else would he be, here? He leads you down the long, perfect corridors, and through great windows the day falls straight onto things that shine, of gold, Saint Isidros and San Fernandos, mirrors in which reflection after reflection moving behind three bean poles there's the same little, plump, leaf green redingote and that curly hair, tricorne in hand; so day falls through the great windows onto the thick, purple draperies, some of them emblazoned with all the Flemish and Spanish lines, the Flemish lines lost but present, the Great Indies lost but present, all the epic bric-a-brac from all corners of the Earth in which kings make their nests. All the ceilings are painted, who cares, he'll repaint them. Goya smiles: so this is all there is to it? Yes; but this is as good as it gets in this world, and in ten years it will all be his. At last, the final fat key turns the final fat lock, this must be it, the antechamber where the Bourbon king dresses amongst quaint paintings, his dead Hapsbugs; the room is poorly lit, it'll be hard to work in here. The prince, who as it turns out is no more than an attendant, bids them enter; why does it seem so somber; there are plenty of big windows in here as well, and daylight; he blinks a little, he lifts his head: he's in a cave, and all over the walls are monsters.

AND HERE, SEÑORA, WHEN the attendant left and closed the door, not one of us knows what came over Francisco

Goya. The linen maids who saw the painters prancing in the courtyard don't enter this place, and the princesses are in Aranjuez, gathering jonquils. Let us imagine then. What would have overcome him, at the very moment when he casually tossed his tricorne onto a footstool and took off his gloves? It certainly wasn't Velázquez, he knew him, he had seen a thousand etchings; and anyway, painting itself couldn't have overcome him because he knew it, too. Nonetheless, paintings were all that was there. What sun went out? What dipped this chamber in dark, light falling in little heaps, while in painting after painting beautiful blues were gamboling, reds and jasmine whites and torrents of pearls, and yet this gray overshadowing the white? It's something immobile high above, you say, but why then does it affect him so, why does all this immobility and exhaustion wrap him up so furiously in deepening shadow, so suddenly? No, Señora, these horses aren't wild, aren't bucking the child princesses and their rattles, terrified and impassive, their count-dukes, terrified and brave, their captains vanquished and captains victorious, terrified: they aren't moving at all, they're just wooden horses. And no, the farthingales aren't turning, nor the little dolls they ring that seem so unhappy, and would you have them dance? So where is all this wind coming from? Not from those dead mountains, those sierras over there, and not from these trees that are as tired as these men, they won't move a leaf during the tempests of Judgment. Perhaps it's this black that rushes and blusters, all this black in foreground and back, all this black that blows by them, pierces them, empties them, this lightness or this lead in the shoddy skin of these painted children, of the count-dukes, of Philippe IV and the midgets he made counts. Yes, you're right, Señora,

God Is Never Through

they are laughing too, these sad sires, perhaps because of all this wind in their blood. That inner wind, it leads us away. But we'll never understand, so we leave. Let us go then, you and I, into this Sevillian cauldron, into this blackness where pieces of princes, of children, are whirling around with a sad king's mustache, a pearl glove, and some Andalusian jasmine; let us go where the name Diego Velázquez is swimming within the fifty crumbling canvases of his corpse; and where little Goya in his leaf green coat is swept up like a whisp of straw, into this cauldron where we read what will be.

He was thirty-two years old, this little wisp, when he was finally led inside. And no one was the wiser for it. Castillo and Ramón Bayeu didn't notice, they were busy sketching Murillos and extravagant Riberas, all manner of pretty pictures, at the other end of what he took to be the king's antechamber but which was something more like the lazaret of a slave trader's vessel on the hundredth day of the crossing, upon the passing of the Frontier, and in which little Goya was preparing to row forever, not with oars of ash he'd once used to apply blues straight out of Tiepolo, but with oars of lead. He looked over at both of them for a little while, his accomplices, over there at the edge of this great darkness, leaning over their drawings, perhaps erasing this line, or perhaps not, perhaps going over it again, passionate and unconstrained, but with an air of authority, the pencil held grandly like a sceptre, a rattle. Their necks were probably already stiff from peering at the paintings above: people aren't meant to look so high; and also they aren't made to release their pencils and rattles, to drink and fall beneath the painted skies, to groan a little and do somersaults in court attire beneath *Las Meninas*. What good are these two, unless you're a man made of paint? Goya took the tricorne from where he had set it on a footstool and sat down gently, hat in his hands, at which he looked. He began to think peaceful thoughts. He thought about a donkey doubtless long dead and tossed to the dogs, this donkey to whom he had, somewhat ashamed of himself, spoken of Raphael, doubling over with laughter and collapsing onto the animal's big ears; he thought about a blind dog that was afraid of Francisco Goya's gimpy saints; he though about peasants in Aragon, the blue beards, about Hapsburg princes with blond beards, about Bourbon princes, blue beards; he thought about muddy princesses and limpid flesh, about the desire one has for women and how it disappears when you paint them, how it becomes vulnerable, fallen, inglorious, so valiant and carefully made up to mask their terror; he thought about an old man from Saragossa who modestly applied a little film of gold between the world and man; about a dead woman who had noiselessly brought hot chocolate to this boy who one day would be painter to the king, noiselessly withdrawing, muddy in his memory, muddy on the earth when she was still alive; he thought that kings are better or worse than other men, if every morning when they get up they need to be buried beneath an avalanche of ghosts. He thought about how far he had come, for this. He thought that the penal colony in Saragossa was about to open all over again for him, but this time without recourse, without a Madrid to look forward to, without a king to give him pardon, without ceilings to poke holes in, without anything. He let all of that spin through his thoughts while he turned the tricorne mechanically in his hands. Finally he lifted his head toward these big, emphatic things that appeared to be men.

Men, without a doubt. Space weighs on us, the earth is old,

the skies are filled with clouds, are as weighty as space; we are between them, we look high above or at the ground beneath our feet, we are elsewhere; sometimes only the finery, the tulle gowns, the uniforms and their stripes, sometimes only they exist, brightening something furtive: a soul, perhaps, which shines intermittently in the little mother of pearl buttons on their vests, along the folds of lace mounting toward some sort of paradise, cascading and playing over epaulettes, and it is to that soul, to its hand that we cling, and which we wear, black and damnable, in our tricornes. But this body visited by wind, what room would it have for a soul? Certainly it wouldn't flee, all this wind holds it there. It's not even a full portrait, its soul is both far above and firmly below on this ground where this soul, as best it can, carries on. On two feet however, like burros that prop their forelegs on a low wall and patiently graze at tender leaves. This body is passionately distant, it doesn't know whether to lean down lower to pick up what has fallen or to tip back its head and beg for manna, getting only rain; it just doesn't know; and so, undecided, it remains there and stares at you, and it should, since you're painting it, but it isn't looking at anything. Wasn't it only yesterday that we were calling that the Fall, Señora? Isn't that it?—some muddy light and the stately somersaults of motionless bodies—is that what keeps falling from these bodies that themselves can't fall because of their farthingales and armor? Do you really believe that it's only the Flanders sky that weighs heavily upon the tired courtesies offered between two rows of posts, from captain to captain? These *Spinsters* are just a painting in front of which the little fatso is sitting, you know only too well what they're spinning, Señora: the bobbins are heavy and full, the women are careful, they spin, they unwind, they cut, all are finishing but they have no end; after one, there's always another. Enough, you say; these empty words are tiring, these big paintings are driving you to your death. Take a last look: at the corner of the painting they call *Las Meninas,* this square of thick air, this haggard room in which midgets stand around, a hellhound waiting calmly, unfortunates who fall forward and old kings in the background like summer mist in a void, the dead Sevillian painter palette in hand, with an undecided look, gloomy as a Hapsburg, distant as Saturn, not looking at anything and pretending to look at Goya in his Sunday best, in May, 1778.

GOYA LOOKED AT WHAT HE would never be able to paint and which for this reason he henceforth would have to paint. If he had wanted to pit himself against what was most impenetrable, he hadn't missed his chance: but whether he had wanted to or not, that was how it had worked out, it had rushed and fallen into the little fat redingote like it had once fallen into the armor of the House of Austria; and he, who didn't have the Sevillian palette that can depict that fall, he had to depict it nonetheless, with what he had, with his Aragonese palette cobbled together from the Venetians, with his minimal understanding and his bluff, where the Sevillian master seemed to have understood everything and had never had to fake it. Because this is how the beaux arts works, Señora: ancestors paint the world, they despair, they know that the world isn't anything like the way they see it, and even less like the way they paint it; but then the grandsons come who suddenly see the world the way the old saw it, and also somehow like they themselves believe they see it, who between the two either fall to pieces or fall silent, fat moths between two lanterns, asses from Buridan, who suffer and who paint. So it went, from father to son, from living dwarves looking to do as well as the dead giants, from the dead to the living, this game of giant dwarves. The prince of the *Bon Retrait,* the quiet Sevillian who now is no more than the shadow of a cypress or the sound of a clock in the gardens of Buen Retiro, Velázquez, walking in the gardens of Buen Retiro, airing his old cloak in the cool of evening, he wanted to make the grade too. And perhaps his personal prince, his secluded master was the painter-duke of Flanders who did bloody sides of beef and women so white, lost in the Fall, growing fat off the Fall, or on the contrary this Greek from Toledo who rowed against the current, who painted so as to fall less, and all of whose flesh returns to its source, is barely flesh, wings, fraises of lace, air and rustling of air; perhaps it was Titian, whose sunbeams are pure gold, or Tintoretto, who made his out of absinthe: and since he held neither gold nor absinthe in his hand, only perhaps a bit of Earthly honey, perhaps that is why he broke down at night beneath the cypresses of Buen Retiro, something that made him abandon all words that weren't sycophantic, that made him eat from the hand of a king and made him accept these mercenary titles, Great Chambermaid, Great Turnkey, Great Master of Palatial Lodging, Knight of Santiago, such that at last he succeeded in some way, he who failed to conceive an unbridled Fall or even the flight. But not even he would admit that; he did what he could; he didn't paint the debauchery of the Fall, or the vertiginous Ascension, those things that only the giants paint; but somewhere in between, men of flesh who wouldn't get to enjoy the Fall, and who all the same would never get to Heaven.

Is this too simple, Señora? He had already seen so many Velázquez, our friend Francisco, so on that day he had neither a revelation nor an abyss beneath his feet. And you say that I haven't talked about the journey he made as a young man to Rome, where he had the leisure to study and absorb everything, Velázquez and his masters, the very best of painting? Of course. You are quite correct. Where did I get this gloomy story about a cave? I was dreaming above this Sevillian cauldron and I suppose I was the one who became drunk from it all when I wanted Goya to be swept up in it, which I guess makes me an old sot. Anyway, you do see him leaving the Pardo at noon, caracoling on his piebald mare? *Salut, Peintre de la Chambre.* And there he is again in outdoor cafés along the Manzanares, feasting, more fond than ever of the *majas* since he is now on intimate terms with the Castilians; see how they dance around him, all these colored skirts rising around him, sitting down with him, brushing against tablecloths, handsome Messieurs laughing, poets and matadors with their joyous gestures in the cool shade, perhaps they're already talking of liberties to come, spoken of in whispers that travel well beyond the Pyrenees. The tricorne is on the table, is matte black; in the full carafes, wine is gleaming. I no longer see Velázquez. Only lilies on water. Tomorrow will be beautiful as well.

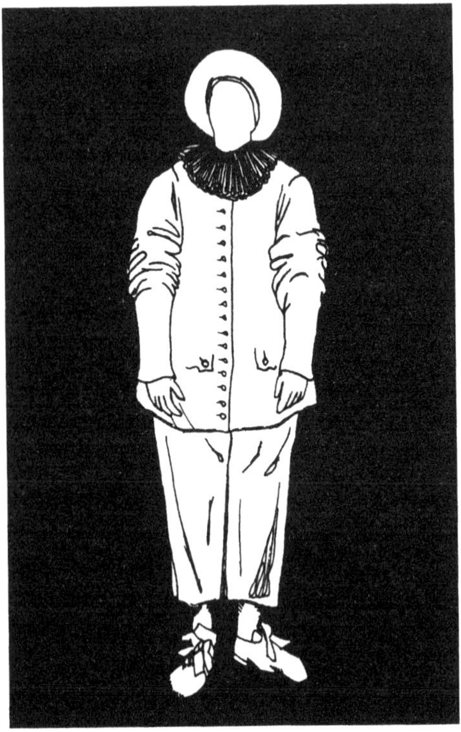

"… Io mi voglio divertir"

for Julien Fischel

In his youth, not to have every woman had seemed an intolerable scandal. But so that you see what I'm getting at—since we can't get at him anymore: it wasn't about seduction; he had appealed, as everyone does, to the two, seven, thirty, or hundred women bestowed upon each of us in accordance with our heights and our faces, our spirits. No, what infuriated him in the streets, in the wings and in the workshops, at the tables of all those who welcomed him, at the homes of princes and in gardens, essentially anywhere women ventured, was that he couldn't arbitrarily decide to have a particular one, a patron's wife, a gamine, or an old trollop, couldn't just point her out with his index finger and have her come and offer herself to him, to be thrown down right there or carried off elsewhere, and be taken. But again, so that you see what I'm getting at: it wasn't about keeping them there, by a law or some other violence; no, what he wanted was for them to want him as he wanted them, indifferently and absolutely, so that this desire made them as wordless as it made him, so that of their own accord they ran deep into a wood, mute, aroused, out of breath, and prepared themselves to be consumed, without any intervening process. That's what he told me, that evening in July, between two coughing fits, and more crudely than I have said: he wanted license; he felt the multiple gift he awaited was somehow due him, but he didn't tell me what debt it was meant to repay, for which he would never be reimbursed, and the enormity of which, the presumptuousness, made him laugh at himself; he didn't bother asking for it; he just wanted to keep quiet, he wanted offerings to this silence; and he wanted for his to have been the only hand in all those dresses, with no more comment than—as sparkling as a spoken language—silk skirts at the frenzied instant. He didn't get a penny—evidently, he wanted too much or too little. Perhaps in that regard he was like all men; my condition hardly permits me to judge and, anyway, I live in seclusion.

I AM THE CURATE OF NOGENT. When I knew him, he had long since given up waiting for his license, and therefore, he painted. Fat Crozat had sent for him, or perhaps it was Haranger, the abbot; those of the beau monde have their peculiar enthusiams here, their Chinese pavilions, their colonnaded groves in which to take meals, listen to violins, to leaves, while watching the Marne through gaps in the trees. So I can't really say which of these great protectors was keeping him, had put him up for the winter in a summery little pagan temple, all terraces and windows, filled with openwork, breezy as a dance hall, which he had given up all hope of heating despite the great fires that burned all day. He went to Mass, perhaps out of habit (I am no longer so certain); I never noticed him there; one morning, after the seven o'clock service, as I was leaving the church, he came up to me. This was before the death of *le Grand Roi*. It was barely light out. A cold wind blew.

He introduced himself, I knew his name; I didn't know his works: I repeat, I live in seclusion. In the dawn light, his gawkiness surprised me. Back then, we hadn't yet taken to wearing powdered perukes; we wore big wigs, enormous morning coats, ribboned culottes, endless skirts and cuffs. The scrawny man who stood before me seemed lost within these rags. Perhaps I hadn't slept very well, but I thought that he didn't look real; you doubted that there was a body within the bundle; but beneath his considerable mass of fake hair, it was difficult to doubt the veracity of a face that wavered between a strong desire to seduce and an even more dizzying need to displease; this made him appear perpetually stunned, feverish, and dumbfounded; it seemed to me that a ghost caught out at dawn would be similarly perplexed, would be similarly eager to make its way back to its dismal home. The wind lifted his wig a little—he had black hair, he was young. His nose was too big. There, on the steps, his hands crossed behind his back, looking down at me from above, this puppet spoke in a friendly voice, a voice with an edge hinted at in his face.

He apologized for the frivolity of his request; he was in great need of a face for one of his big canvases, a face like mine; and when I exclaimed how unremarkable it was, how ordinary, how it was as likely found on a curate's habit as on a musketeer's collar or on a porter's shoulders, he impressed upon me that this quality was not so common in a world in which musketeers and porters believe themselves to be out of the ordinary, and take great pains to make such supposed dis-

"… Io mi voglio divertir"

tinction clear. He insisted, charmingly, flattering me with explanations of how deplorably dull I was; he tempted me nearer while keeping me at arm's length; I couldn't tell if he was poking fun at me, at my face; whether it frustrated him or pleased him. He was smiling, but he still seemed baffled by something; it wasn't me, at least I don't think it was, I was so predictable, so taken aback by his aplomb but at last giving in to it, at last accepting to be his model. Abruptly, he said good-bye and moved off with long strides through the dry wind. I forgot to say that he was tall.

My face was painted over two mornings, in the icy little temple I have already mentioned. The painting was all but finished before I had even arrived: it was of a tall Pierrot with his arms at his sides, standing there stupidly. What can I say? I haven't any ambitions now, but on my way there I had hoped, for once, to find myself in the pose of prelate, or perhaps as a prophet, and I would have happily settled for a minor part in some big sacred painting, a Levite trailing Joad or an obscure witness to the Passion, rather than for the powdered lead he wanted me to play. I remained dumb before this big white thing; he pretended to suddenly notice my embarrassment, which, apparently, he had expected; he apologized grandly—laughing—and I did my best to laugh as well: my face was supposed to be anyone's, and anyway, who would recognize it in the homes of the gentlemen where our painting would be hung. I posed.

I saw a leafless landscape through the windows; I saw leafy landscapes on the walls, painted, autumns and summers in arbors, on banks, sudden sunlight and secluded shadows, as though sealed tightly beneath clusters of trees one wouldn't dare enter; before them were beautiful women with their backs to us, perfectly postured, with long naked necks, dresses rising and falling back to their feet, dresses as closed as the shadows of the woods. Something like the world. I was surprised that someone would devote a life to such things, to faking things and not quite succeeding at it, and when one succeeds one only adds one ephemera to another, what one can't have to what one doesn't; and yet, to this game of coin and counterfeit, some give themselves over completely.

I told him this; he laughed, offered me sarcasm in reward for my great insight, and then went on muttering to himself. While painting, he spoke little but cursed often; wore neither wig nor hat, but a nightshirt that seemed out of place; wiped his brushes on his stockings; I should also add his bafflement, his thinness; in a word, he looked like a painter, the way most people imagine painters to look, as I imagine them myself: vain and true, full of pretension and seriousness, and maybe the pretension really is seriousness, that only this pretension can convince them they are painters, only it can make them paint, pastorals or masterpieces, farces or Apparitions; they too must see themselves as coin of the realm. And mine was far from an exception to this rule.

No matter. Now he's dead, the little charlatan: he's not minting much of anything, even if some flirt swoons in front of his fine draperies or laughs at my sad face in the café that the actor Belloni opened, where anyone, they tell me, can now see it. Was it for this that he had worked so hard? All this industry, to seduce whom? He could afford to have his air of astonishment, to fight with nothing like some Quixote, to throw his colors, brilliant or muddy, into the air, onto his stockings, his furniture, and in the end to stop suddenly as he often would before one of the paintings underway, baffled. I

"… Io mi voglio divertir"

don't want to describe him at work very much; just know that he skimmed across the canvas with brusque little strokes; little movements; that there wasn't a part of him that didn't participate in this nothingness; that the sweeping whirl of his whole arm, his whole leg, released violently with relish like a whip, always tapered to a furtive little touch, an exasperated caress, as if stymied: hovering in the air above the canvas, he would muster a despotic paraph that would somehow become a trembling little cross; he would wind up for a tremendous slap in the face and leave nothing more than a beauty spot on the cheek of a Columbine: all of this troubled him deeply, drained him. I imagined that all painters were like this. It wasn't until later I learned from his lips that this little touch, like fencing, wasn't so common and gave him the distinction of being classed by his colleagues amongst those they call, in the jargon of the craft, *les petits toucheurs*.

So was this Pierrot hurried forth. At the end of the second morning, the painter turned his back to me and stood looking out a window. I looked at the thing. I saw something like a man from the Eighth Day—God, exhausted, having forgotten man had already been created the day before, and for this one there wasn't another Eve in the wings; I recognized my dull face in those features; and I recognized his by its stupor, and more so the surprise, the resignation of someone who had painted for nothing, again; the face of anyone and no one when we think no one is watching. It didn't speak, it was either a ghost or an idiot, all white, with huge, manly hands; in the background, Italian poplars and pines, a scarlet stooge busy doing something and ardent summer mists, all blue: some other summer, doubtless long ago. On the grounds, the winter wind whistled in white gusts. He watched the wind.

I DON'T RECALL IF THERE WERE any women in that painting; it didn't seem to me there were any in his life that winter—although one of the servants fat Crozat or Monsieur de Jullienne had left him was pretty and sly, a bit more affected than one might wish. So it was to distract him that I dragged him along on walks to the frozen carp ponds, even though it was hard for him to keep up with me, not having a real taste for wilderness or nature, and for long walks even less; perhaps it was to distract him that I told him about my life, while he kept his pretty much to himself; some have said he was taciturn and it is true that he was; but he talked—about fat Crozat, or handsome Jullienne and his little silver knickknacks, his brocaded vests, his ties, about his masters or about the little people of Nogent who raise rabbits and chickens, who gossip and die—he was a little rogue, alert and kind, mordant, mimicking them all artfully and sparing no one. A buffoon, but a ghostly buffoon nonetheless; because what he taunted most and what he made seem the most unreal of all was himself: he, *Monseigneur le Peintre,* before whose shadow he pretended to doff his hat, affecting a Picard accent and opening his eyes wide like a *Jacques de la farce.* It was again to offer him some distraction that I invited Agnès and Elisabeth, the daughter and niece of one of my bourgeois friends, both of whom were often overcome by fits of giggling, love letters, and feigned melancholy, overcome above all by the pursuit of someone they could love, innocent but ignorant, milky, cousins. This was to offer him some distraction, but my heart isn't so pure: it was also to tempt him.

He was working on a large composition that had been commissioned by the Academy or some dealer, I don't know which anymore; I don't remember the painting very well: all I can see is a high forest and white clouds collapsing though

"... Io mi voglio divertir"

it, through a sizeable break he had opened with his brushes and filled with clouds all white, all the way to a little temple vaguely like the one where he was painting, but ghostly and reflected in the water; women stood paused before this break in the woods, as usual. The countryside had already been painted, the figures were only sketches; he reluctantly asked if Agnès and Elisabeth would like to be these women—he seemed annoyed that they were there, was perhaps politely exasperated, and he couldn't keep his eyes off them. Of course the two girls couldn't keep quiet, were blushing and sneaking glances at each other, but not saying no; he had some elegant outfits and few that were ridiculous in which he costumed his models as it suited them; he went through an armoire and came back with armfuls of crackling silks, pink and blue satins, ball gowns and corsages. They found themselves suddenly marquises, they clapped their hands. They got dolled up in the next room, still giggling. We didn't look at each other. He arranged them as he saw fit; they were seduced; I believe the painter by whom they had initially been intimidated didn't take very long to disappear from memory, making way for someone less distant, for sweeter secrets, for a tailor ready to serve them, consumed with draping their little bodies in silks, or for a hairdresser who trussed up their tresses and placed a feather atop the trembling mass, revealing their ears and their necks, their cheeks appearing fuller and their necks nearer, as expected. He did some rapid sketches, standing, crouching, sitting; almost always from behind; they lent themselves to this mise-en-scène with an affected good grace. He, disgusted, sketched in three colors as if these delicate hands were just some landscape, these little shod feet.

A landscape, really? He was very nearly trembling; it wasn't from the breeze and he knew it. He was more serious than ever, too serious. They were taking his breath away; in the presence of these little, eerily costumed hearts, aglow at being seen and at being at his mercy, he became someone else, his taste for farce disappeared, he lacked every word: all that remained was an intense reserve that seemed comic to me, a sort of total bodily embarrassment, a stiffness in his spine and his arms that left only his right hand free, unfettered, prodigiously free, and as brusque as ever, as distorted, stroking thick and fast. He seemed watchful, but you couldn't tell whether he was exulting in having his prey within reach or conjuring it in vain. He paid as much attention to me at this point as he did to the furniture; I had disappeared; he only spoke to one or the other, in few words and rather rudely, to have them adjust their posture, to look at him or bend their necks away: they were praying, I think, that the way he was acting was only the terseness of a fine artisan, while it was really the exasperated, hidden sigh of a famished ogre sharpening his knives under the table—but of this I wasn't certain until much later, and neither were they.

They returned often: they were taken with him or by the pose he held them in. I was no longer present for their encounters; but I know he used the cousins for several paintings, or at least I have since been able to recognize them, Agnès blonder and Elisabeth plumper, happier, with a more imperious neck and a sharper laugh, delighted. I wasn't around in January, business with the bishop dictating a journey. I wasn't back in Nogent until the end of March. One night—nearing the days of the Passion, night approaching, raining as it rains at the end of March—I paid another visit to the painter.

"... Io mi voglio divertir"

The grounds open out at the top of a little valley sloping gently toward the Marne; the house is halfway up the incline on the right, near groves that partially conceal it; along the length of the cloister to the left, the royal road dips toward *pont de la Marne,* which one does not see from here, beneath a double row of hazels; between the house and the road there is a vast expanse of open meadow, a virgin meadow that borders the sky, which, in summer, looked like those in his paintings. The rain beat down upon this meadow, the low sky crushed it, night fell from beneath it. I was drenched, I felt old. I was as far from the road as I was from the house, on a rise above them both; through this sheet of rain I saw a door blow violently open down below, rattling windowpanes; someone ran out onto the soaked earth, ardent but clumsy, as girls are wont to run: it was Elisabeth in blue satin, undone, dripping, whom I recognized as she passed within feet of me, without seeing me, into the middle of the virgin meadow, beneath this dirty sky; the water beat down upon her trussed-up hair; the feather hung down against her cheek like the wing of a dead bird; she was looking up at the empty sky, crying, her mouth was wide open in something resembling a laugh; she lifted her dress with both hands and stumbled heavily, falling to her white-stockinged knees onto the muddy grass. Far behind her, Agnès followed, walking quickly, not running, her cloak wrapped around her head; it seemed to me she was calling to her, that she too was either laughing or crying. The two silhouettes appeared desperate and passionate, outlined against the sky. The rain fell harder. The sound of galloping off to the left made me turn my head: on the royal road, disappearing and reappearing behind the rows of hazels, horsemen in uniform filed ceaselessly past toward *pont de la Marne,* greatcoats filling with wind, heads held close to their mounts' manes, horses and riders as pallid as the sky: I thought I saw the great pale cross with its fleurs-de-lys flying like birds, like night: gray musketeers, undoubtedly, blind on their heavy horses, charging brutally beneath the downpour toward a harbor where they could dry boots and feathers at hearthside, just as they would have unsheathed swords in battle. The shadowy greatcoats disappeared suddenly, their hoofbeats collapsing away like the drums of armies long lost, languished and beaten by the rain in Flanders: the storm won out, the brutal scene was swallowed up, the girls were no longer there, the catastrophic field was ready again for the violins of summer. He was standing next to me, immobile, his wig dripping down onto his coat. He looked at me, mouth wide open, and suddenly began to laugh, interminably: my arms hung at my sides, I stood there like an imbecile; I tried to smile, and the shame of all this overwhelmed me. I didn't ask him anything.

HE LEFT IN SPRING. HE GAVE ME the little drawing of a woman sitting, lifting her head, and seeming to ask something of someone whom we cannot see, with a lively, downtrodden look, perhaps on the brink of tears; it could be Agnès or Elisabeth, or any other. And of course he gave me this gift with the same disgusted air he always had when his eyes fell on one of his products: his execution was inferior to his inspiration, he believed art was something far above what he practiced, but you would suspect as much. So he carted his disgust at being *Monseigneur le Peintre* somewhere else; a barouche bearing Jullienne's coat of arms took him away just when the weather turned beautiful, taking with it too his

"... Io mi voglio divertir"

black humor and his pranks, his trunks of props for the women he painted, his big wig and the smaller ones they had begun to wear during that time, his frames, his phials of oil; perhaps he looked at the vibrant acacian foliage, at the little temple, all that he would no longer paint. He didn't think he would see me again.

I remained in Nogent, and soon after his departure I found I missed my painter, his leaps of humor and maybe even the way he abused me, or at least surprised me. I didn't bother with the beaux arts anymore; I was back at the card tables to lose a few louis, back at Mass to ensure that the world kept turning, back at the gossip of the bourgeoisie, their momentous problems over their daughters' betrothals, and back walking with their daughters by the carp ponds during fine weather. As for the cousins, I no longer spoke to them about the one we had known, for his name made them blush—and I don't know if it had to do with certain tender pleasures, with shame or with tears, perhaps both—they turned away; I wasn't their confessor, just a tiresome acquaintance who loved women more than his uniform permitted, someone deserving little credit: and I don't deserve much, I, Charles Carreau, by chance the curate of Nogent, whose true face was perhaps revealed over two mornings one winter, ignorance made flesh and dressed as a zany, forever turning my back on the poplars, an ass, and a scarlet harlequin, toward whoever might look at me, bravely, on a few inches of white and some linseed oil. I certainly didn't know what had happened, that night of anger and rain, of horsemen, one March.

I do know that he went back to his native Hainaut, where he once again saw the little low wall, little cousins whom he had drawn and who had grown up, streets where no child painted; I know that the varnished tiles his father made didn't seem like very much alongside the work of a Rubens, or perhaps it was just the opposite; I know that he went back to Paris because the dresses rustle more there, the princes are better spoken, and renown is less discrete; I know that he took walks through *les jardins de Luxembourg,* for although he didn't particularly like nature, you needed to see it if you were to paint it. He slept chez Vleughels, Crozat, Gersaint, neither staying long in one place nor marrying a soul; he perhaps had an adventure with an Italian pastelist who sent him letters from the Florence, Rome, and Naples that he did not know, letters sent to *Signor Vato;* but certainly he painted scores of whispering women, women sighing while thinking about something else, women who said neither yes nor no; and before them, men planted valiantly, strumming their theorbos in vain. They tell me his works were hung on *pont Notre-Dame* and were admired by *le Grand-Monarque;* that everyone smiled at him, and that his great show of good spirits was only show. I know his fury earned him his lungs, that his black humor took up residence there and became that cough, black and short like his *petite touche;* I know his exasperation with having to paint was only compounded by that of having to die; that the scandal of not having every woman became that of not having had them all—all the more intolerable. But I'm ignoring how he seduced them, reduced them, or suffocated them; no, I don't know what form the tempest took when his models' smiles became something else, nor what happened to them in the ateliers, beaten down or terrified, fleeing into the rain, when perhaps the whole

"… Io mi voglio divertir"

world—rustling, filled with beautiful skies and great industry—becomes a cavalry charge, disastrous hoofbeats in the night, something you can't paint.

He returned at the end of the spring of 1721. This time, Haranger had sent for him, Haranger, the abbot; had sent for him and would soon be rid of him, would abandon him there, where he would no longer move princes to pity nor cough on the naked shoulders of marquises, but where he nonetheless would be housed like a prince, because certain grand things—the beaux arts, the nearness of death, a well-known name—dictate a bit of consideration; he was housed in the most beautiful house in Nogent, a rocaille palace with fountains and grounds and terraces, all beneath a swarm of golden leaves; it was Le Fevre's summer house, Le Fevre whom no one ever saw there, steward of *Menus Plaisirs du Roi,* an intimate of the Orléans; it was a palace on the Marne. At first, I didn't know that he was there.

I met him one midday on the road to Charenton. It rained hardly at all that summer, and April had already been dry; on the dusty road I saw a dusty little valet carrying tripods and easels on his back, cumbersome paint boxes; my heart tightened, I thought I could smell a scent from long ago in winter; there was someone sitting beneath the apple trees, hunched over. I had them stop the chair, I descended; it was he; he lifted his head and watched me approach, mouth wide open.

The pink shade of the apple tree fell over him; other shadows softly surrounded him, firm and round, vast and rustling like painted dresses; blue skies reigned, burned into the new leaves: everything, this time, was as he had painted it, everything except for him. Old age, which he painted little and to which he doubtless had given scant thought, had taken him early; he wasn't forty, he looked sixty; it seemed cruelly appropriate that the great fatigue won of so many painted pleasures would paint itself on his features. Beneath the silk of his morning coat, beneath the rigor of his stockings and the ribboned ladder of his tie, everything cried out of the final debacle: he was bag of bones, with sinister, clownlike wrinkles ringing his eyes; his big nose stuck out extraordinarily; his hair was white, like the wig resting on his knee: a ghost once again, but in daylight, and sweating like a sick man on the sunny road to Charenton, far from his icy home. The big, unsatisfied eyes began to smile, to laugh, he rose with a painful somersault. He was happy to see me.

He did the whole "Your Eminence" bit, just as long ago; he started out volubly, still dumbfounded but this time feverish, in every sense of the word. He told me he'd had his fill of Crozat, Gersaint, Jullienne, who were small potatoes anyway; chez Le Fevre he was cherished like a Persian, served like a Mongol, a sybarite; he told me that he just painted the expected little things so as not to lose his hand, little landscapes, little marquises, little fools, all the hackneyed work he could draw and make dance with his eyes closed, the little interminable minuet; that if His Eminence deigned to come by he would find himself in good company, with so many Pierrots around; that he eats late, since life is short; that now he was steward of his own *Menus Plaisirs, Monseigneur le Peintre*. He laughed; he threw himself into an imitation of Le Fevre, affected, pretending to use a snuffbox or to wield some porcelain bauble, chattering away as Le Fevre would to the accompaniment of an absent oboe, peering at the shadow of the little dears of whom the other was so fond. I laughed. He stopped in the middle of his routine, livid, bathed in sweat,

"... Io mi voglio divertir"

as though he had remembered something momentarily forgotten that had suddenly come back to him like a blow to the chest or a woman running off—but this one had neither body, nor name, nor dress. He put on his wig, he said goodbye to me abruptly, leaned on his valet; he was coughing; I offered him my chair, he stammered out an excuse and then, with a grand, derisory gesture to the surrounding countryside: "Trees to paint, Your Eminence," and with disgust: "Trees!" He headed off with a hand on the shoulder of his dusty little flunky; weightless, the pink of the apple trees flew across the blue sky.

CHEZ LE FEVRE, THINGS were sinister. The sybarite lived on bread and onions; the Mongol was served only by his little paint-toting valet, who also half carried his master when he lagged behind, and who would be made to hold a cello or wear a harlequin's hat, who soon became pigment and who soon looked as though he wanted to say something, he too, this valet who spoke little and meant even less; as far as girls went, I saw only that servant whom Crozat had given to him long before and of whom he had not rid himself, though she didn't lift a finger; she laughed in hallways while applying her rouge and slept beneath trees on the grounds, exasperating him: you didn't have to be a sorcerer to divine the nature of their relations. In the salons, the mannered boudoirs, and the bedrooms of the north wing that only he occupied, he had piled everything pell-mell into the corners—furniture, Chinese bibelots, snuffboxes, and mother-of-pearl knickknacks, his easels set up everywhere, his colors ruining the tapestries: it was all a studio to him, put together in monument to this lost but incurably paintable world, and he painted with a growing urgency, this time quite real, with all his old furor, this time well founded, the expression of which was either in a perpetual eruption or was in a slow release endlessly deferring the inevitable blast, *petite touche* after *petite touche,* fit after coughing fit, little rigadoon after little minuet that the plague-stricken bravely dance rather than succumb then and there, blackly, mouths agape, buboes bursting: but we didn't see them fall; with a whisper, they asked the name of a certain tree, of an air, lifting their dresses between two fingers and pivoting into the next step. And so, inside, with all the windows shut in summer, with the thick fumes of hellebore and borage that the doctor from London had prescribed, with the stink of spirits and oil, in this unbreathable hospital where stubborn little marquises, lunatics all of them, smiled unbearably from ear to ear, whispered from canvas to canvas—inside this little palace his cough reigned supreme, unfurling across ceilings that Coypel had designed and experts had executed, cabinetmakers, painters, brigades of specialists, the cough climbed the stairs and banged around in the attics, bloomed in the shower of light, banged on the windows, perhaps called to the sun, but no, it never escaped, it just shot a bit of purple into the purple paint of the autumn poplars; it was prisoner too, hurling itself outside yet nonetheless trapped there, caged in a throat, sad as a broken theorbo. It remained in the palace of Le Fevre, beneath the sun of 1721, in this great box, beating this white stone drum beneath the trees, killing him from within.

It drummed on for three months. In Paris, much is known about this period, and I don't mean about the daily visits that I paid him, which I hope were helpful to him, although charity wasn't the only thing that drew me; it is known that he

"... Io mi voglio divertir"

reconciled with Pater, the unruly companion, who spent a few weeks there amidst the fumes and the petty proselytizing about painting; it is known that he, who was going to die, gave the other, who he thought had little talent, the gift of being treated like a painter; that Crozat and Jullienne came, Gersaint, Caylus, jumping out of carriages into each other's arms, leaving with bundles of enigmatic canvases under their arms, stiff under their wigs and in their bearings, but not unpleasant; it too is known that the flesh painted during this period remained as pink as the skies remained blue, because death can manifest only in crude effects, in rot and in a peaty palette that he hated, or on the contrary in depictions of the Assumption that tend toward being too bright, violet irises rimmed with chrome yellow, which wasn't his style and which perhaps he hated as well; it is known that he worked himself to death, as they say, because he had to sign off once and for all on his little corner of renown, signing with that little live part that still remained. And it is believed that the glory that came so readily and never departed would have repaid him his pains, and that he would have had only to await the glory of death. But nothing is known about the day he showed me the extent of the debt the world hadn't repaid him, which he had clandestinely tried to make up, silently, with a counterfeit coin of his own minting that did little to pay it down; nothing is known of the kind cellist who had been stolen away; nor is it known that he died like a beggar, a creditor held up to ridicule who choked on wicked thoughts while two steps away from a treasure he couldn't bring himself to surrender, and out of which he'd been cheated.

He had fallen asleep in a blue sitting room, downstairs; he

had fallen prey to one of those terrible coughing fits that threw him fully dressed onto the nearest bed where he lay shaking for hours, this impassioned cough breaking him apart. He caught his breath a little; there was blood on the lace of his collar; he panted between the mirrors, his head tipped back, lost. I had to help him, and I knew very well that pious exhortations would have little effect on him; I don't know why I thought to praise his paintings, I who am in no position to do so and who until then had made no such effort—and anyway he never asked for an opinion from anyone about his work, he would always interrupt, with an assurance that seemed either offended or derisive, as I've already said. So I talked to him about the pleasure his work brought me, the illusion of depth in his paintings, his marquises. How could I not have noticed before how sick he was with pride? He was half sitting up on his elbows and was looking right at me; without a doubt, for the first time I interested him, I was something other than that fool he liked, that priest he made fun of, I was easing some of his suffering but it wasn't enough, it would never be enough. I played the good apostle, I assured him that in the end he had succeeded at feigning the world; the crudeness of such a lie appalled me. He sat bolt upright, he looked at the birds fleeing in trompe-l'œil on the ceiling at top speed; he laughed, curtly, which didn't surprise me. He whistled between his teeth, without anger: "Is that all?" Then, as helpless as a child, plaintive, "And my reward? My wage?"

He was the best-paid painter of the time. That he lived like a hermit was his business, whether out of coquetry or greed: but he could have afforded a white palace all his own, and trees under which he could have coughed to his heart's con-

"… Io mi voglio divertir"

tent, could have spent his princely wages on a deathbed, some of the money thrown at him year after year by Gersaint, Jullienne, the Orléans. I refused to understand: I looked at him questioningly, without a word. He seemed to be hesitating; something childish fleetingly enlivened him, like long ago; he got up with a jump that should have exhausted him, and from his morning coat he took the key to the south wing and handed it to me; he was trembling; "Go see for yourself," he said; and with a sort of tenderness: "I wonder if Pierrot has ever seen what he will now?" He firmly pushed me outside; I turned around to wait for him, he gave me the sign to go alone; from behind me I heard another coughing fit, and then the door of the box was shut tight, the cough rattling at the windows briefly, ceasing.

This air of mystery, this key straight out of Bluebeard, had prepared me for the worst, for some sort of villainy. I pushed on the door of the south wing, and strolled through the boudoirs: I saw no crime, only libertinism, a lot of it, and some very beautiful paintings he had done. It wasn't much of anything, really; just some very naked women, at their moment of pleasure, large and vivid, turgid like Rubens, playing luxuriantly on a carpet of dresses and fallen leaves, deep in a wood when before he had only dared paint its fringe. Just female flesh made pure light, exaggerated, and eerily undone; and of course he had also depicted, incidentally, what gives them pleasure, the futile and aggressive part of man they want, that falls prey to their excess; but he would have done better to have limited himself to the inflection of a neck, the bend of a wrist, a leg in the air—these were sufficient indication of the extent of their joy; the painter could have forgone what was too often apparent. These ravishings had faces;

they were the same women, the same as always, those few that run through a life and upon whom desire happens to fall, the Agnèses, the Elisabeths, and Gersaint's wife, all the wives, the daughters and mothers, the scatterbrained and the sullen, an Italian pastelist for certain, a servant with simpering airs; but these weren't exactly the same women; because these were held aloft by the graces of a somber man leaning into them, a maestro whose profile was merging with the foliage, enough in shadow that flesh had become light, a ghost or a thing of the trees, but if he had turned toward us, perhaps we would have recognized the big nose and the offended look: he had them. He had them? Was it he with his little touch and his incalculable desire; was he both cause and beneficiary of these thousand little deaths they wouldn't die? He had nothing: they were still running off, ruthlessly held there they were escaping, both the little servant whom he'd had and Gersaint's wife whom he'd not, Elisabeth whom perhaps he'd had, subjugated and had, terrified and had, scandalized and not had, and who cares whether he had or hadn't laid his hands on them, since they hadn't dedicated their drunkenness to anyone: he wasn't the Sole Proprietor; and there, routed by his attention, his desires, his touch, they pivoted, they offered themselves over to nothing, again, to the wind and to the land, to the coming evening, to the tumult of their lips, the convolution of their loins, with all this white highlighting their eyes and their stomachs. They were fleeing. And it wasn't with little pirouettes anymore, little lying whispers that make the rounds during minuets, those *mayhaps,* those *see you anons,* those *we shall sees* that tirelessly ricochet through rural gatherings *en concerts;* it had become the final refusal, the *right away,* the *now,* and at the same moment a cry, which

"… Io mi voglio divertir"

surely burst forth and shone brightly, rose straight up to the tops of the trees as if midday itself had cried out, and it had to have been midday that had cried out, because nothing was there, no one, neither he who was the superfluous cause of this pleasure, nor she who was its extravagant effect; and the one who had cried out, who had finally stopped talking, who had finally stopped thinking she was somebody, a dress and a name, Madame de Jullienne, Mesdemoiselles de Jullienne, Elisabeth or some cheap slut, the one whose features we recognize—the full cheeks and mouth, the long neck and throat—she sank away at the instant of her cry, disappearing, becoming this superlative creature, exalted and ferocious, who in various flashy frocks was always the same and was all of them, was interchangeable, unnatural, this undifferentiable Lilith who gnashed her teeth and fainted away, more imaginary than angels, but like angels was given glorious body and fabular flesh, and like them let out a sort of exaggerated song.

I hear whispering across his grounds the wind, the promising, incompliant little mouths, the rustlings of satin. He needed all that—the little gestures, the words and the satins, musics. He smothered this cry with all of it. Underneath, he painted that cry. This cry or this prodigious silence that reigned in the south wing, the intense cry women make that we hear at the beginning, in terror and breathlessness, when we appear in this world that never makes good on its end of the bargain.

I left; it could have been six o'clock, the afternoon was beautiful; the air was thick with the scent of lindens; at the edge of the neighboring meadow, two horsemen in greatcoats were chatting; the evening sun caught their plumes, on their young shoulders the great cross and its fleurs-de-lys were bluing in the shadows like wings; they had dismounted from their horses and, with one hand on their saddletrees, were peacefully watching young girls singing in the meadow.

> *Let us go to Cythera*
> *on pilgrimage, two by two.*
> *Each will find her pleasure,*
> *in amusements sweet and true.*

He was still coughing in the blue sitting room. He told me what little he had to say: that in his youth, not to have every woman had seemed an intolerable scandal. He was thirty-seven.

HE QUICKLY WORSENED. He had no illusions about what was happening to him, this obstinate rejection of the air we breathe, this renunciation of air, this *no* said a hundred times over and as peremptory as the ecstatic *yes* of the women of the south wing, the *no* incarnate that lips no longer said but that a body shouted, a chest, with the burlesque nodding of a head that made one believe that the one who was coughing was saying *yes,* saying *yes* all the way to the grave: it would take a smarter man than I to say which air he was coughing up, which amongst all that he had breathed, the marvelous, poisoned air of his Flemish youth, the air that touch upon touch blued the summers of his paintings, the air that with a single touch from above blued the ponds in morning, in summer, the blonde wind of gardens maundering around necks, chignons, sudden gusts of wind on our cheeks when you lift up a dress deep in a wood, the time it takes, the time he had taken all the days of his life, in all the paintings of his

"… Io mi voglio divertir"

III

life, which was another time altogether; the glorious air in Paris when you discover that beneath its skies Gersaint is using one of your paintings as a sign; the triumphant air in the courts; the heavy air in the garrets; the stinking air in London where they tell you that your illness is called consumption, that is what you are coughing up, when you suspect that it's actually called painting, or the world, or women. Smarter than I, whoever could have made out which it was, the world or painting, that he was coughing up, or perhaps their unbreathable mix; whether it was hellebore and borage that his lungs were driving out, or the Veronese greens; or all of it on top of the rest of it, the recollected air of everywhere and everything painted. But I can't say; I'm not a doctor, thank God.

He didn't leave the blue salon. You needn't much space in which to die. There, the second Sunday of July, toward noon, he asked me to destroy the canvases in the south wing, as he was too weak to do it himself. I didn't want to; since I had been going to see him, I had become intimidated by all the labor in his art; I saw them as exhausted, delicate, more fragile than living things. So I refused; the anger I expected didn't come. He told me in a tone of great fatigue that his fame had to remain well bred, even if he hadn't remained so himself; that what had been the published backside of his unknown work—the little minuet, the oboe, courtship, and dresses—had turned out not to be the backside, but the front, as far as everyone was concerned, perhaps even as far as he was concerned; and that the fronts, the originals, his wicked and ecstatic paintings on the backs of which all the rest had been painted—thrown like dresses over haunches or verbs onto tongues—no longer existed and didn't deserve to survive any more than the cries of newborns or of the dying, the mysteries of midwives and of *punchinelli:* that perhaps it was little more than that, painting, a game of dress up. And only this game deserved to endure. He bequeathed his little chamber musics; it didn't matter much to him whether or not we heard the echo of the fugues he had played only for himself: whether he had played poorly or too well was of as little interest to him as was the incorporeal Being who stirs our paintings and perhaps accepts them, who looks at them, who amidst his choruses still reserves an ear for our music, who knows that flesh is too much for us, isn't enough for us. To angels his harlots, to man his marquises: he wouldn't visit this terrain again. He said again, and the anger was building in him, that he wanted to have them one last time, in fiery deliverance.

I burned them.

It took all the middle of the day. The little valet helped me, brought them to me one by one, departed; I don't know if he had already seen them, but he looked at them as long ago he had no doubt looked from the pantry at the dinner tables, a myriad of candles and truffles, teals, champagnes of white gold. I lit a great fire on the warm stones of the terrace, near the lindens, in front of the blue salon, and into this fire they disappeared. After three the sun reached the terrace, and they rose in this light. They crackled; there were no flames to see, there were no sparks, in the white air the sun burned brighter; it wasn't much of a sight; it was just a little earthly sacrifice in a frivolous palace, nothing momentous, just a midden of unwearable old clothes in which a tired old fellow, an abbot or a peasant, all blackened and bent beneath enormous bright lindens, poked at ashes all alone as it burned until nightfall.

Perhaps he—sleeping in an armchair behind the open

"… Io mi voglio divertir"

window in the shadows, wearing a tie for the ceremony, a wig, white gloves, and red velour hat, all decked out and as ghostly as ever, disgusted and gaunt, far from his home if he had one—perhaps he saw it differently: surely not what he might have wanted one to believe he'd see there, some flaming harem of theatrical agony, the shadow puppet of a king with a big nose; perhaps he saw the Assumptions he never painted, perhaps in chrome yellow and azure; a celestial assembly of fields, a little fire, two men, no living women; certainly he saw cousins he'd caressed during a childhood in Valenciennes; or perhaps just what was there to be seen, what he had always seen, preserved at least once, at least in the sign he painted once for Gersaint: unknown men taking paintings off a wall, stuffing them into dry wooden crates next to tinder about to be struck, entombing them, and some dubious old fellow scrutinizing the painted flesh one last time before the window closed, the Marquise to end all marquises already leaning on his shoulder, holding her lorgnette like a scythe. Watteau leaned closer on a few occasions to see what was burning, lifting himself halfway to the window, his red outfit, his wig, blazing in the sun; then disappeared back into the shadows, dumbfounded. He said: *that foreshortening is worthless;* he said: *no one would want those;* and he said: *that Pierrot doesn't matter;* and later, in a strong voice, a neutral cry: *Marie-Louise Gersaint.* The old disgust beat on his lips. He coughed at length, covering his mouth with his tie.

At the end of the day, the little girls returned to sing in the meadow; the last frames burned on the embers; perhaps they saw this exhausted old man, living chez Le Fevre, who was burning litter or old clothes. They didn't see the king with a big nose, his red clothes in the shadows. They were holding each other's hands; they passed from shadow into light and their dresses were changing; their song in the lindens seemed as heartbreaking as the smoke of a work that was burning down; I thought about my youth, about the uniform I wore, opportunities I had missed. I watched them for a long time. The little valet took me by the hand, showed me the window, laughing: he had fallen asleep like a good little boy, his nose in his tie, cradled by these songs after the carnage, like a warrior, like a child.

> *Let us go to Cythera*
> *on pilgrimage, I presume.*
> *Young girls rarely return, O no,*
> *without a lover or a groom.*

He died on the eighteenth. Early in the morning a storm gathered. Nothing stirred, stilled trees in a white sky. The storm didn't burst, nothing came. In the interim, he wandered: he said that he had never painted bad weather; he said that his painting was gay; he affirmed that he too had been gay, at great pains propped himself up on his elbows, begging me to agree with him. Yes, I told him, he had had nothing but joy, pleasure. The storm took its time; he wanted a crucifix; I offered him mine, which is cheaply made but artful enough for the good people here, for their final glance; I prayed; he made a sound like a laugh, the crucifix fell: "Take it away," he said. "Can one have so poorly served one's master?" Then: "Your face is enough for me." This last bit of coquetry moved me more than I am able to say. There were a few thunderclaps, no wind; stone trees began to lean toward *Monseigneur le Peintre* like taciturn monseigneurs; a flash of lightning carried off the scandalized little rogue, in the falling

"... Io mi voglio divertir"

afternoon, at the hour when dresses begin to assemble on the terraces that the fountains besiege, the innumerable leaves.

Toward seven, the rain began to fall. The trees resumed their old palaver; Watteau was cold. I left him to the servant and her tears, to the astonished little valet. On the grounds, beneath the gray sky, on the road to a little vicarage, I saw neither girls nor musketeers, saw no choruses, saw neither panaches nor girandoles. Birds were leaving trees, returning to them. The skies were changing, neither rain nor sun repaying us. Who pays our wages? What master counts such coin? I hear the laughter of his young girls, and the others, his women, I hear them crying. Perhaps they await their wages too. Now, I'm alone in the world; I'll die one of these autumns. Autumn is coming, the world will yellow; processions of girls leave each morning with baskets of fruit, with amorous schemes, with their dresses and their rouge; they laugh; they wriggle in scarlet frocks; later in the day, they lie undone at the feet of trees; I, lagging behind this procession, adrift, too tired to go on, I'm not walking any more, I lower my arms and peer out, at you.

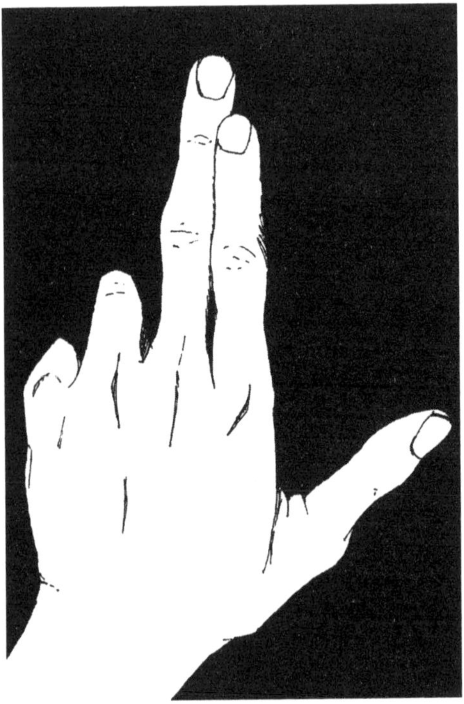

Trust This Sign

Vasari, that is, the legend, tells us that Lorentino, a painter from Arezzo and a disciple of Piero, was poor; that he had a big family; that he never rested; that he painted on commission, from nature, members of religious committees and parish priors, merchants; that undoubtedly he fought feature after feature to capture these faces of men of gain, striving to attain the merciless indulgence of Piero's hand and scarcely succeeding; that on occasion he did not have a commission; that one brief February at the far end of the Quattrocento, no one knows in what year since Vasari doesn't say a word about it, the disciple didn't have the wherewithal to buy a pig. Nonetheless, his little children begged him to kill this pig that he didn't have, as was done at this time of year in Tuscany and elsewhere. They asked, "Without money, how will you manage, Papa, to buy a pig?" And Lorentino, Vasari tells us—fifty years later, from the comfort of his sprawling baroque palace in Arezzo, his little Vatican born from a hand as poorly suited to painting as it was ideal for writing—Lorentino told his children that one saint or another would provide for them: he probably said this because he was both pious and stoic, because he indulged in Hope or wanted to challenge this invisible, immanent justice, the disappearance of which is the final deception in the lives of disappointed artists; and because Vasari, a painter without genius but a delicious writer, was a romantic. So came the feast days of Saint Antoine, Saint Vincent, Saint Blaise, and whether via theological virtue or authorial fantasy, Lorentino repeated this prayer to Saint Antoine, Saint Vincent, Saint Blaise. As Mardi Gras approached, the saints had yet to show. And since the family was preparing to celebrate the fat feast with beans alone, and since the beans were already on the fire, a farmer appeared in this poor neighborhood of lower Arezzo and knocked on the painter's door: to fulfill a promise he needed a portrait of Saint Martin, but to fulfill payment on this portrait he had nothing more than a pig weighing ten pounds.

The scene is pleasant and seems to come to us from a simpler time. Vasari doesn't describe it. It was after dinner. The farmer had spent the day being shooed from the various studios in the upper part of town, where he had been pushed around and humiliated; he didn't look like he had come from Arcady; his leggings had slipped to his knees; he wore a little wool bonnet pulled down tightly past his ears; he was somewhat corpulent, with a redness in his cheeks that comes from working outside all the time, like a permanent shame at having to work outside all the time. He was around forty and exuded the expected mix of amazement and wiliness of those born in the country; he grumbled in the street while searching for this painter who didn't even have a sign and who had been suggested to him in desperation or as a joke. It was cold; in the great, bright sky above rushed winds from the Verna, with snows, and this weather was getting under the farmer's collar, making him stoop a little. Lorentino opened the door: he was corpulent too, was also wearing a bonnet, but was older than the farmer and of course was short, as his name implies; his bonnet was red. When Lorentino spoke, he found himself short of breath—the cold, the stairs, the anguish, age; but he didn't have to talk much since the farmer—with the wealth of explanation and the genius for digression that dealing with city dwellers brings out, the fear of not being understood, and, more profoundly, the anguish at being in the world without having enough words to bear witness to it—the farmer launched into a long, hazy monologue. He spoke too quickly, in loud bursts; he stood on the step to the doorway, the wind from the Verna lifted little wisps of hair from around his hat; he was holding a long lead at the end of which was a pig—or perhaps he carried it in his arms, because ten pounds isn't heavy and we really want it to weigh about ten pounds, a little pig. Lorentino was looking at the pig. While the farmer spoke, Lorentino eyed the pig.

THE WIND FROM THE VERNA had taken what little breath he had in him. He was hearing bells. Nevertheless, through these hazy ramblings he could imagine Saint Martin interceding, in person, in the life of this farmer whose mother was some old Maria whom the saint had cured of a long illness that had kept her moaning and groaning; he imagined old Maria dancing around after pigs with her cane, since Saint Martin's heart and his efficacious hand that one never actually observes aren't reserved for the dukes alone but for old

Marias too; and he imagined that this little pig had been their largest, that the farmer had nothing better to offer Saint Martin: the saint and the old woman came out the most vividly in all this talk, they danced in the midst of it. Lorentino well understood that this farmer both loved his mother and believed, however vaguely, in the somehow too-efficacious handiwork of saints: this didn't surprise Lorentino. But behind it, behind the wobbly dance of mother and saint, the farmer was doing his best to explain something yet more surprising; something that he wasn't accustomed to naming. Who can say where he had gotten the idea, by what metaphors he had made sense of it, because we're no longer in the Quattrocento, we didn't leave before dawn for the city with a pig in our arms; but somehow he had gotten the idea. And we have no idea how he had become possessed by the magic of images, deep in his countryside. He expressed this after a fashion. The painter looked at him for a moment. The painter understood that, because of some peculiar hierarchy imagined in the wide fields during squalid work, the farmer, far from images, had deemed them important, had elevated them to a place of grace within his own somewhat suspect personal pantheon; and while watching his mother die, in his helplessness he had promised the saint, without thinking, something so beyond his grasp, so remote and impenetrable, something princes purchase for the price of a farm and that is executed with colors that cost half a farm and still remains out of reach, even if one has an entire principality with which to pay: a portrait, an object resembling a saint, a painted thing that would once again give the saint flesh, if he wanted to give an old Maria a little more life. And certainly the farmer hadn't believed, he hadn't held any hope that the cure would take, the yokel, because he wouldn't have indebted himself so immoderately. Such a debt astonished him.

He stopped suddenly, at the end of the few words he'd used and which he'd been arranging for some time now. The smell of beans rose from the house, he remembered that he hadn't eaten since dawn. The pig's eyes were jumping from one thing to another, indifferently, terrified. The old woman and the saint moved off, dancing in the wind; Lorentino looked at them, then at this man who looked a little bit like him, then again at the pig. He accepted immediately, or at least, as soon as the man had finished this story that during the day he had told a hundred times in the studios of Arezzo, as soon as, dumbfounded, the farmer had stood there at a loss and had waited, looking at the painter while saying to himself at least this one had listened to everything he'd had to say and hadn't interrupted him; when Lorentino accepted the farmer immediately felt contempt for him, believing he was being duped and therefore not trusting him, or perhaps—if we indulge in Hope as well, we too—he thanked him, on his knees. And we can allow ourselves to think that gently but firmly Lorentino had helped him to his feet, as in his master's frescos old Solomon helps the queen of Sheba, although between these men it was about neither love nor kingdoms, although they both were getting old and a little fat. So it was agreed. The farmer moved off into the countryside while talking to himself, perhaps with a bowl of beans in his belly, perhaps not, but without his pig. The wind made him dance a little too. Night was falling.

We do not know if Saint Martin witnessed the scene, and if he had, whether he might have stood closer to the farmer or to Lorentino.

Lorentino considered all of this in the big room down below, the studio, holding the terrified beast that hadn't much time left, that wouldn't look indifferently at the world much longer. He asked himself if he had enough pigment left over from the last commission; he decided he had. And the motif for this preposterous commission, to which he gave thought prior even to killing the pig, scarcely required a second thought: he decided that he would do the saint at the expected moment, when on horseback or on the ground he cuts his cloak in two and offers the beggar a half worth all heaven; and, of course, Roman, warriorlike, armored. But as models for these two figures, their resemblance to men, he was not yet sure. First he thought of giving the beggar his own face, and the saint that of dead Piero; but something in this idea made him ashamed of himself. Keeping himself in the role of the beggar, he thought that the saint could have the face of the farmer, twenty years younger; he felt ashamed of this idea too, a painter doesn't need a farmer. So he resigned himself to being absent from this painting in which he wasn't of much use, and decided to give the saint his master's face, in his prime, on his scaffolds in San Francesco amongst the Constantines, the queens of Sheba, when he was already forty but would look younger in the memory of an old disciple; and so for the beggar, the wily, dumbfounded face of the farmer. But maybe he would do something completely different, it hardly mattered. Lorentino was a little annoyed, was trying to avoid these rapid little eyes looking up at him; he heard the wind whistling outside. He didn't start on the painting that night, he had to kill and dress the beast first, which he did.

And Vasari, regarding the details of this miraculous little

skit—which was more out of the old Flemish masters and their beasts, their gifts, their more clement God, and their cold country than out of the Platonic dispensary where he painted too-plump Virtues and helmeted young boys in the employ of lascivious old men—Vasari doesn't mention the particulars of these culinary operations. He stops there. But in his *Life of Piero della Francesca,* where our story is told in ten lines, in a little aside about the faded face of Lorentino d'Angelo, which didn't warrant the ten or twenty little pages necessary for the unfurling of a *Life,* Vasari leaves it as understood, or rather says nothing about it as though it goes without saying, that the old disciple was happy about this little miracle, was dazzled and aware that a saint had offered, in the flesh, a pig to his children for Carnival; Vasari leaves it as understood that the painter thanked his blessed art for another triumph of theological order, Golden Proportions, and the way of the world, all of which had manifested in a pig; Vasari leaves it as understood that Lorentino cried tenderly; that proudly he had produced this pig before his children. And that they all had fallen to their knees. Vasari leaves all of this as understood.

One can disbelieve Vasari.

HIS MOTHER HAD NAMED HIM little Lorenzo, since he wasn't growing quickly: Lorentino. In this inner theater in which we play the leading role, not always the lead, but at least from time to time, in order to survive—he appeared under the name of Lorenzo. Lorenzo d'Angelo. But he bore this name only for his own use; the neighbors and the commissioners always called him Lorentino, even though they didn't mean it in the same way his mother had, they didn't say it sweetly, nor spitefully either, they just said it plainly; which was only fair. His mother was dead, his hair had gone gray, and he was usually out of breath when he spoke, but the Aretinians always called him Lorentino and it is fairly certain that he recognized himself in this name and answered to it. It's only fair, thinks Lorentino, and you can see him, sitting in the upper room, surrounded by his family, having taken off his bonnet to think. It's a domestic scene in chiaroscuro, and Lorentino, who learned *la pittura chiara* from Piero, has no interest in this half-light. Everyone is preparing the meal and he, for a moment, is resting. The frozen wind from the Verna whistles louder past the windows; in his street, beneath the dark cypresses, the farmer runs through the black. You see night following behind him along with the remains of day, following behind him like dogs, one black, one white. The children are smiling, they thank their father for not having lied, they've gotten what they wanted. Lorentino is smiling at them, thinking of something else; he is asking himself about this little Lorenzo and what had been done with him. And so he looks at Angioletta, his tall and beautiful daughter who is still with them, who doesn't yet have a husband though men revolve around her like shadows around the sun. And little Lorenzo asks himself, or perhaps it's Lorentino who asks Lorenzo, why this perfect object sprung from his loins hadn't instead come from his art; why neither the pleasure he'd had within Diosa nor this flesh fallen from her hadn't transformed Lorentino into Lorenzo. Without speaking, he asks Angioletta which sacrament addresses the art of painting and how it may be used to gain a better name than that which one is christened; this he asks Angioletta, who is painting made flesh, but who isn't paint.

The wind whistles; in the light of the great fire Angioletta sits across from Lorentino. Without speaking, he asks: What will remain of you, beautiful face? A soul? What mad law drives us to possess this nothing in moving bodies? Why can't you remain eighteen years old for an instant under the fleeting midday light, beneath the shadowy lilacs? And why didn't I know how to paint you—you—not your excitement at soon having meat on your tongue, not your features that will change once you leave here and a man has had his way with you, but you, your youth, your force, your unfettered soul, when you were twelve years old, when you were fifteen, while you are eighteen, royal in the midday mist, gloomy like midday, brilliant like midday, like all the ones like you whom he painted up above, on the scaffold, in the shadows, whom from the opposite wall I could see while I did my touch-ups, my clumps of trees, my icy highlights on icy Oriental hats, when I was fifteen and watched him work, watched him not looking at anyone, watched him remain endlessly still and at last rise with his hand extended before him, drawing out from within a limestone wall—a wall that itself wasn't miraculous, that we had prepared with our own hands before he arrived, kidding around just as you would have expected, Luca, Melozzo, the others, and I—thus drawing forth some Revelation, massive theological maidens, Angiolettas more real than you who bears this name, servants, but servants who serve only light made flesh, the king of midday, because the midday mist and the hand of Piero had made it so. My own hand isn't good for anything but killing a pig, painting a peasant saint for a peasant. A saint with the name of a bear.

He would have preferred Saint Francis, Saint Augustine, or Saint Jerome, of course, or a cleric in a cardinal's hat. He rose: Bartolomeo needed his help and was calling for him. Bartolomeo lived with them. He was the only apprentice, his only student, all that remained of a studio that had never flourished anyway. The disciple had a student of his own now; but he didn't want to think about that. He hadn't taught Bartolomeo very much, although he had taught him all there was to know about the profession, the tricks of the trade and the Florentine theory, how to mix plaster, how to mix ultramarines with lime and to read Alberti; that it isn't life, but art, that one must search for in painting; that you shouldn't make backgrounds gold; that scenes of earth should convey the same idea as those of heaven; any number of mathematical trifles. But all that really counted he hadn't taught him; because what counts isn't conveyed with words, it is observed and, like the midday sun, wordlessly overwhelms anyone who sees it and remains forever in the body of an apprentice who watches you do nothing for hours until suddenly you rise, extending a theological hand that blesses the wall with a single stroke, and once again sit, meditating, frowning, discontent, perhaps that's all painting is, the perfection of a gesture and instant Revelation; and discontent that this gesture that has just impeccably brought a face to close—a pause, an *élan,* a midday cloud over the queens of midday—isn't accompanied by the trumpets of Judgment, ringing out in a little church in Arezzo, tossing disciples to the ground while you yourself fill to bursting with the dimensions of the universe, eardrums bursting and limbs lifeless, but God in the flesh beating in your heart grown suddenly too small for Him. He hadn't given Bartolomeo the responsibility of being a master. He had spared him this image from a sweet dream or a nightmare, from a sweet dream and a nightmare that pulls you forward toward weightless things, shows them to you, prohibits you from looking elsewhere;

and as for the passing shadow that steals your taste for bread, which perches on your shoulders with the weight of every painter interred since Zeuxis and all their tombstones, so much weight that weightless things seem almost in reach, but they move too quickly, you can't seize them precisely because of this great weight beneath which you labor and which spurs you to seize them; this ghost one drags all the way to death, which during its life dragged along its own, its own that you thus drag part of as well, as Piero dragged Veneziano, had been embarrassed and driven forward by it, this Veneziano that Lorentino hadn't known but whom Piero venerated and therefore whose carcass and tombstone Lorentino carried along with Piero's; and who knows what names there were beneath Veneziano, Lorentino didn't know these names, but he felt the weight of the stones upon which the names were engraved. Bartolomeo wouldn't have ghosts at his back, not even horsemen saddled with tombstones; he wouldn't be a good painter. But Lorentino—who bore Piero and all the armies of Constantine, Heraclius, their armor, the miters from the Orient, the cavalry, and even the struts for Milvius Bridge over which they rode—for all that, was Lorentino himself a good painter? My poor Bartolomeo. Lorentino looked at him for a moment; he was nearly a farmer, he too, short with short hands; he came from *la Pieve a Quarto,* from nowhere, he had more of a taste for Angioletta's shapely limbs than he did for Golden Proportions, and he was too full of good will. No, Lorentino didn't have a student. An apprentice, just so, a lieutenant more nimble than he and that's all, younger and more naive, who prepared his palette and colors as though he were cleaning tripe for blood sausage.

Lorentino had faith in the arts, perhaps even more so than Piero, since Lorentino never really succeeded, and yet made it his life; since he never tried to start over again; since he suffered from not knowing how to start over; but he didn't suffer when, finished in all their glory, the frescoes hadn't brought down the walls of a little church in Arezzo, didn't open a great breach for the cavalry of angels. And Lorentino was perhaps happier than Piero, if one can measure such things. The wind whistles through Arezzo, through the night, striking the walls of the chapel of San Francesco within which paintings are in shadow, invisible at this hour, gray and fallen like ashes, ignorant of everything, of the wall that bears them and the hand that had thought they could bring such walls down. The chapel stands tall in the wind. The farmer still far from his home jumps a stream, the Tiber; he misjudges his leap and lands with a foot in the water, splattering into the blackness, he swears and continues on heavily, unhappy about this world that whistles through the trees. Lorentino, whose hand had long ago touched Piero's hands and remembers them well, thinks about this farmer, about Bartolomeo the Obscure whom Vasari doesn't mention, about San Francesco in the blackness.

Diosa, his wife, had been beautiful. She had retained her unwrinkled brow and her big eyes; circles beneath those eyes made one think that the soul of a dreamer remained within her old body. She still knew how to smile, and would until she died, probably, as everyone does. Lorentino kept the rest to himself, her toothlessness, her stoop that drags the spirit down with it, the two sacks hanging from her chest, Eve leaning on dying Adam. Diosa was helping Lorentino; together they were cooking this blood in big pots and were adding what spices they had. He quickly realized that only his hands were fussing over the meal; he raised his head: Diosa was standing at the end of the table, leaning against it, the rest of her body weighed infinitely down but upright, her eyes lost but widening at what she was searching for within, and deeply at that, those things one doesn't quite find and which depart. Her hands hung empty at her sides, she seemed extremely weary and disenchanted, was searching in vain for what reasonably could make sense of this fatigue, this disenchantment, whether through some payment or some end; but no, Lorentino clearly saw that she wasn't finding it, her spirit beating behind her eyelids, looking everywhere and bumping into everything, the pleasures in life were behind them now, those she had clung to and those she had ceaselessly postponed: Lorentino had lost the touch he once had with her, she no longer had the body that summoned such a touch, and when she was young she hadn't had the rich dresses seen in dreams, dresses that display a body that one hides when it grows old, and she wouldn't have such finery, since Lorentino no longer got commissions; each day that came drained her all the more, for even sleep is weary, it no longer restores; she was looking for something she could put in place of her hopes, put in place of all there is to look forward to, tomorrow, when one is twenty—love, dresses, all the exhilaration of being twenty years old. It was beating its wings, this bird, this soul, it was falling from the nest: they had a pig and so it seems that there is a heaven, but that wasn't really enough for her either.

She noticed that Lorentino had stopped what he was doing, she looked at him. A passionate kind of pity passed between them. Lorentino once again took refuge in this old glance that made him feel both shame and pardon for feeling shame. Her own eyes too had seen Piero, from below, from a little chair in the church where she had waited in vain for his hand to touch the wall and the trumpets of Judgment to burst forth; but below Piero's sullen expression her twenty-year-old eyes had also seen the painter's fine doublets; and she was thinking then that her little love who on the opposite wall had been fiddling with hats in uncomplicated shades of blue and highlights on armor would wait passionately for the same thing, would fight the same way, would call forth the trumpets of Judgment the same way, in vain, of course, since this is but the bluster of men who've let a few too many of those azure backgrounds go to their heads; she thought that her little love would too have fine doublets; that with this vanity, this pretension, this sulkiness, he too would be celebrated and showered in the gold of the courts, at Urbino, at Rimini, with the Holy Father, that with his failure at setting the trumpets in motion but his success with the princes—a noble failure serving as guarantee of coin in his pockets—he would offer her dresses and servants. She was well out of it now. Again Lorentino heard something resembling bells, now nearer. He thought back to the story of Saint Martin.

PROVIDENCE, he thought, can't suddenly decide to deceive us.

He grew accustomed to this idea, thought about its every sorrow. He even got a sort of satisfaction from it, an arid comfort, the same felt by children one punishes by not opening the door and who instead of seeking shelter remain beneath the rain with wild eyes, jumping up and down in the puddles, getting covered in mud while crying, but who are drunk with tears. He saw himself as a little child undeserving of such a destiny and relished it. The volleying bells ring loudly and suddenly stop: beyond his illusions—illusions of this Providence that on one hand can do anything and on the other did little for Lorentino—in all the silence, Lorentino saw something very far away. It had to be a memory, but it was surfacing after years of forgetting, a memory so forgotten it was coming out new, real, still, paused before his eyes like a little corner of a painting. It was morning, in the Siennese countryside. The sky was pure. The dew was gone, the hour when the cypresses had drunk it had passed, they had taken it into their great black chiffon, rustling, twisted, had tossed it up into the pearly blue. Around nine o'clock. The cypresses had calmed. The red earth was cooking. On this ground the color of hell that cracks apart but is nonetheless from this world, because it bears shadows and footsteps because it is beneath the sky, there was a beautiful bunch of grapes, crushed on the ground, before which Lorentino was ranting and raving. But he couldn't hear a word of it, there was only silence, he couldn't remember. He was twenty-five, he was pointing at the grapes, taking the sky as his witness and gesticulating. That's what he had first remembered, his gesticulations. He was alone in this violent expanse, in the company of cypresses. Not entirely alone: at nine o'clock forty years before, squatting on an open bundle of disordered belongings, Diosa, head bowed beneath the sun, saying nothing, was on the verge of tears. She was looking at the ground, at the grapes. Lorentino, by his fire in the night in Arezzo, also looked at these grapes, saw the crushed pulp mixed with the Siennese earth. What was going on? And why was Diosa on the brink of tears? He had made only one trip to Sienna, and he had returned with a heavy heart. And this had to be the trip.

He had gone to secure a very coveted commission, on Melozzo's advice, the little colleague who also had mixed plaster for Piero, and who now was a painter; there were a lot of hopeful painters there; Melozzo got the commission. This was inexplicable to young Lorentino's heart: immense hope had seized him when the red city of golden painters had risen up at the end of the road, had filled him with all things Siennese—the sky, the purple-shadowed streets, the joy before Sassetta's lillied arabesques, the women, the saints, the stones of the roads—all this richness that he had within him that his eyes alone released from the world—all this wasn't enough to make him that uncommon painter who secretly existed, a master whose emotion the commissioners should have divined, and therefore his savoir faire, his burgeoning talent. Was it that Melozzo saw the Siennese light and women with more emotion? Propelled more love toward Sassetta's flowered saints, had more heart? Without a doubt, since Melozzo had gotten the commission. Lorentino remembered that the magistrates had barely listened to his proposal, had quickly called in the next painter, a Ferrarese who couldn't have been considered young but who did have that apocalyptic air, young and uncompromising, like hunger; he was a great one; he had looked with such wrath at this pitiful young painter who was on his way out. Lorentino again saw this face perfectly before him, this face held in reserve in his memory for forty years that hadn't come forward in as long. Fleeing the *piazza da Campo,* where already the trumpets were heralding the selection of Melozzo da Forli as the magistrates' choice, Lorentino had cried, leaning against the uncompromising wall of San Domenico from which one sees the whole city, Diosa holding his shoulder and saying something sweet to him from time to time. The bells of San Domenico were ringing at his back, were leaping against him, in this noise Sienna was dancing, climbing straight for the sky as if a great knife had cut the city in two, the length of the ramparts, and had lifted it up toward the mouths of angels. Sienna wasn't for him. He remembered having thought that it wasn't worth loving these cities beneath the sun if no one was paying you to paint them, there in the distance, perched firmly on the hillside but rising high into the sky, behind a saint or a donor. And all of a sudden in his tears he had seen the Ferrarese pass before him, the old gothic painter who hadn't gotten the commission any more than he had but who was walking, with a stiff step, with each step irascibly hitting the ground with his cane, and for a moment he had glimpsed this young man who was crying, and then had left the city all alone by the northern road. Then and there, Lorentino had stopped crying.

He thought more about the Ferrarese, about pure anger, youth. He thought he remembered leaving early in the morning from Sienna on foot as they had come, walking and not painting, passing through the suburbs, Diosa buying some grapes for the road; he liked grapes, and while buying them Diosa had looked at him, him, with that air both intrepid and imploring that the poor have when they're a little extravagant at the worst times. This poverty had exasperated him. Dawn was bright at the outskirts of the city, then across the countryside; he was walking in front of Diosa and was violently quiet; he walked quickly along the red footpath, Providence before him with its back turned, just as today. And when far from Sienna he had wanted those grapes, when his thirst had added to his bitterness at not being the best of painters, at being unworthy of seeing the dawn and not even being able to count on Melozzo—Diosa, the scatterbrain, had taken these grapes out of her bundle where she had carelessly stuck them, crushed, inedible, as if when she was trailing behind Lorentino, thinking about her love for Lorentino, she hadn't had enough room left over to tend to what was becoming proof of her love, in her bundle, this fruit bought to console Lorentino. She had tried to smile, but not for long: perhaps she too had thought then that Providence couldn't suddenly decide to deceive us. Lorentino relived the penitent shock that had erased this smile. She had wanted to sort through what remained, he had snatched them from her hands; in this fruit, which he had brutally thrown to the ground, he had seen the world and had cursed it. In this ravaged bunch of grapes that was as vivid as memory, he saw the world: bells over a city that wants you to leave; Piero painting too well and nonetheless dying, who moreover was dead, because his eyes had filled with those spots that were white on the outside and black within, that had arrived instead of the trumpets of Judgment, a little valet leading him by the arm and helping him walk, sitting him in the sun in a street of Borgo, his theological hand extended before him, so as not to run into the walls, blind; it was a world where Piero's hand worked and nonetheless you worked with a different hand; it was a world that made you want to paint even when you weren't the best, where you still had to paint since you hadn't learned how to do anything else, no matter that the only reason you had tried was to become the best; it was a world where the skies part in order to give you a pig instead of Pope Sixtus's chapel in which there's a great ceiling to paint: it was a world in which you are born and you have to die, something that manifests for an instant, in a little object, in a little something to eat; there was a world in those burst seeds, and in their bright pulp that the sun was already withering, under the ants. Lorentino had heard the black bells of hell; and in a moment of bedazzlement, a drunkenness straight from hell or perhaps even from this world when it shows itself too clearly and then blinds us, Lorentino had insulted Diosa. He might even have hit her. She deserved it for having come with him to Sienna in her prettiest dress, the only one that was presentable, for having waited all alone near the communal palace and for having rushed forward when he had come out with his head bowed, for putting a bold face on things with these grapes that were boldness, when he himself hadn't any boldness left. That was it, a trip to Sienna; and it was the only trip they had made to Sienna; and when later they spoke about it, when they remembered, they recalled the beauty of the city and the fineness of the weather, the youthfulness that had since left their legs, but they hadn't spoken of Melozzo, nor of the scorn the magistrates had reserved for Lorentino d'Angelo, nor of the bells of this hell whose very sound is black, nor the grapes on the red footpath, nor the little ants that were eating them. Because you have to go on. No, he never returned to Sienna. He hadn't traveled very much. Florence, he'd never dared go there, he'd held on to the dream until he was thirty, perhaps forty, but only on the days when he had succeeded with a detail, a bit of a city, a blend of colors, but he didn't think about it any more, only good painters go there. Good painters have to prove themselves. Lorentino hadn't proven himself in too many places. But once, he had gone to Borgo, to his master's.

The meat was cooking, it was now a matter of time. While

remembering all these little trips, Lorentino was also watching these figures moving around him, a man, women and children, his disciple, his family. They were casting shadows on the walls. These shapes are said to resemble God, and yet He casts no shadows. The wind whistled outside, shadowless, arriving from the Verna, this wind that long ago, high up in the snows, had surely pierced the hands and feet of Saint Francis, this wind has its piercing rays too, like ice but invisible, and one could perhaps paint it with a halo as well, a very long halo for such a wind, but over what head? He moves through the countryside, strong and irascible, arming battalions in the trees, a cavalry of lances in the poplars, walking on water, caressing it, spurring it on, holding it back, like a horse. He has dogs, one black, one white. The farmer is running along near the Tiber, afraid of this great horseman riding across water. "Saint Martin, good Saint Martin," he says. And old Maria who is somewhere waiting for him says the same words, she hears the same wind. Behind the walls of San Francesco, Constantine's horsemen are at peace in the black, are invisible, no more real than the wind. Constantine has only a little cross, he isn't afraid in all this black. He doesn't hear the wind.

He had gone to Borgo. It's not as far as Sienna; but it was well past Sienna in time; Lorentino had grown fat, he grew easily winded when he walked, and so greedy had he become with his breath that he ranted and raved no more, and cried less and less. It was neither ambition nor legitimate aspiration that had pushed him to make this trip, but perhaps a little Hope despite it all, although not for himself: he had brought along his oldest son, whom he had named Piero and of whom he wished to make a painter. Piero di Lorentino. And Piero di Lorentino, already a painter in a way, was working in Foligno for an illuminator, he copied the same old motifs that had been copied for centuries, he drew big uncials on which he made ivy grow, lilies, and all around the old texts he carefully scattered good young kings in the springtime of their reigns, little rabbits we hunt and that seem happy we do, that gambol right under the hatchet; he scattered fortunate martyrs dancing together in great rounds, gamboling into their pots of boiling oil, onto their stakes, their crosses; and angels, with trumpets. Yes, little Piero was making his living as a painter, but not quite how Lorentino had hoped when the child had begun to paint. So he had brought him to Borgo to see what a master was, have him get a sense of it, and so the theological hand could settle upon the ten-year-old head of curls and perhaps do with live flesh what it had done with dead pigment, which is to say ennoble it, make it real at last and sure of its reality, and though that flesh would still walk on two legs and fill with varied desires, it too would fill with the triumphant certitude that we are made in the image of God. And of course he also wanted to show him, his eldest son, that Lorentino d'Angelo—his father who looked like a nobody, whom the princes didn't call and whom the prelates took on only when three others had canceled on them, who painted patron saints in country churches—that his father made informal visits to great men, stood with and chatted with a man as famous and better paid than Saint Francis, although without the pierced hands or the halo around his head. He was awaiting a mix of many joys from their visit, something difficult to put to words. And he did it out of pride, in other words, Hope. He had been told that the old master was blind, but that's a misfortune like any other when you have a body of work behind you like his. It had been at least fifteen years since he had seen him.

It was nearing Easter. Father and son were experiencing the simple joy that springtime offers when one leaves early in the morning. The earth rang brightly beneath their steps; this emptiness that the sky conceals, there are faces there, perhaps your mother's of long ago, or what remains of your youth, and what remains of it is vast. Beneath trees that are yet leafless but full of song, Saint Francis preaches to the birds, and the Revelation redoubles their song. The father and son move from shadow to light, then back into shadow; for a moment, everything is bright: they pass amongst these early blooming trees, perhaps almonds, which are as light as air upon air and beneath which shadows dare not stray. Little Piero's face was filled with these things and too was unshadowed, was only more pink. He walked with great seriousness; it was as if he were pondering a great project that made his features seem resolute; he took pride in this grown-up trip from which he expected some sort of great advent, so much had his father spoken to him of it: he was hoping for a reality more real than this one, whose portent he felt all around him amongst the almond trees. Little Piero was strongly drawn to this stronger reality. When they saw Borgo, white trees in great numbers made an airy crown around it. "Piero" the child repeated to himself without moving his lips, and this name already within him was also rising from the immense place where our eyes meet the sky, was singing there like fifty monks together in a church, but all in bright frocks, like plumage. These flowers and these voices came from this name in Borgo, they shuddered around it, weightless and strong like flowers. And he, Piero di Lorentino, had the same name. The father watched him out the corner of an eye, knowing what the child was thinking, and he knew that any moment, before his child's eyes, he would be speaking to the legend, he would embrace that name. His cheeks too were rosy and shadowless; he too heard the singing of these blue-frocked monks. They entered the town toward noon.

The master wasn't at home, they were told that they would find him in a piazzetta up above. They made their way.

The piazza sloped downward, was deserted; from far off Lorentino saw him at the other end, sitting against a little wall on a projection of stone in front of a sort of market in the shadows, but he, Piero, was in the sun. His shirt was blue. Lorentino, who was walking at his customary pace, had the impression he was moving very slowly. The piazza was treeless, but many pigeons were walking around it, you could hear that silky noise they make when their fat bodies rise into the air. It was only then that the disciple really thought about the master's blindness: Piero couldn't see him coming, and that's what made it seem as though he were moving so slowly. Piero was visible and expressionless like a thing or a painting. Nonetheless, someone did watch them approach: sitting on the ground against the legs of the blind man, little Marco di Longaro, the valet whom the magistrates paid to guide their genial relic through the streets, observed the arrival. Piero was sitting rigidly upright, his head cocked to one side, warming himself on the stones as old people do. They now were before him, the sun beating against Piero's white, wide-open eyes; his head was still but his hands were moving, one searching for Marco's shoulder, questioning or nervous, the other rubbing the stone seat with its fingertips. Lorentino noticed immediately how much he had aged; the skin on his neck was withered, his veins were protruding from his hands; but it was still he, the square head and the great jaw, sullen, but no more so than before, perhaps less so, and the strong frame that nothing had stooped; all of this was just beyond those plaster eyes against which space inarguably collided. Lorentino thought that Montefeltro, Malatesta, the great captains, had been afraid of those eyes, in a sense, when those eyes had watched them pass into posterity. Sigismondo Pandolfo in his war harness had been afraid of this old man. Lorentino felt a very sweet urge to cry. He announced himself. Piero seemed not to comprehend right away; the tips of his fingers came and went across the grain of the stone: "Ah, Lorentino," he said at last. "Little Diosa." His voice was far away, tranquil, the same as it had been in Arezzo when he hadn't been angry. He leaned forward a little and Lorentino, who was very moved, did as well, embracing him clumsily, since he hadn't dared or thought to take him by the shoulder to direct this kiss. Piero's skin was cold. "Is that Diosa with you?" he said. Lorentino responded—he stammered a little—that it was his oldest son, whom he had named Piero and who would be a painter; and having said this he pushed him a little toward the blind man. The child didn't move, he resisted, serious and sullen, as if insulted: he looked at the dead eyes, and even more closely at the sleeves of the handsome Spanish shirt that bore long scratches and streaks from the plaster, from filth, since the master, not seeing the walls, had to rub everywhere along them. The child didn't want to get anywhere near him. The hand of the blind man lifted, remained extended briefly in waiting, and since nothing came, fell back down. He smiled, he said that it was a good first name, Piero, that he himself had born it without displeasure, and that painting was a fine profession, but fatiguing. He asked the child how old he was, and the child responded angrily. The old man fell quiet. For a long moment there was only the sound of the pigeons; Lorentino didn't know what to say; he had a strong desire to cry. He knew perfectly well that the master couldn't see him, but he didn't dare look at him; he was looking off into the somber little market behind them, this wall with a view of nothing. He thought about the high walls of San Francesco. He asked himself if in all the black beneath the plaster spots on Piero's eyes there might be enormous figures on those walls, great maidens, God the Father, or perhaps only wind; doubtless a little bit of everything. Once again he looked at the master, but below his face, at his shirt. He told him that he hadn't changed at all.

And so they spoke a little about what they had in common, the profession of painting, faces of yesteryear; those of Arezzo from the time of the frescoes, of Melozzo and Luca who had both done well, who worked for Pope Sixtus, of Perugino who had done even better, and of him, Lorentino, who after all had nothing to complain about, it wasn't going so badly, he was painting; not for Sixtus, of course, but you can't have everything. He laughed, and the master laughed too. Marco and little Piero were making faces at each other, the bigger of the two had taken out a game of knucklebones. Preoccupied, the child didn't look at them again; Lorentino once again saw the rosy face in the almonds where Piero's great name was blooming, along with all those blue voices, singing. Something like remorse squeezed at his throat. At last he said that a bit of business had brought him to Borgo, a matter of an inheritance, that he shouldn't linger; that he was happy that luck had allowed him to see his old master. The master seemed moved but said nothing. Lorentino embraced him less clumsily this time, he got a good handful of the ample shirt at the shoulder, of the rich stained silk over old flesh. When they were at the bottom of the piazza Lorentino turned around; draped in the empty space, the old man sat impassively beneath the pomp of midday, blue shirt shimmering; a girl passed slowly through the market: disturbed by the dozen, pigeons took wing, rising from beneath the awning above Piero like one great mauve body rising, climbing, dispersing. Once again, Lorentino felt as he had upon arriving, before seeing a blind man and not knowing what to say to him, triumphantly hearing the great name of Piero calmly spread through the applause of so many wings. On the way back, the child ran in front of him and didn't look back once, and Lorentino, short of breath, looked at the ground. He hadn't returned to Borgo since. He didn't know if the master were dead.

THEY WERE EATING SAINT MARTIN'S pig. The smallest children, already full, were clambering into the laps of the adults. Lorentino wasn't completely lost in his journeys, his memories, he was also enjoying the feast; but he felt ashamed, even though he was smiling at Angioletta as she served him, even though he told Bartolomeo to save some of his energy, they would have work tomorrow. The wind was still with them, was roaring incomprehensible words into the skies above. No, Saint Martin shouldn't have done it; it was a joke at his expense. The sacred one should have taken pity on his art, not his hunger: and anyway, art, when it's given to you, when you can execute it perfectly and that's what they pay you for, art always gives you something to eat, at the end of the day. It fills you up in all sorts of ways. Angrily, Lorentino turned away from Saint Martin.

He dreamed of a fairer miracle. He thought about Saint

Francis high above in his snowy retreat where the wind is from, where the stigmata are from, Saint Francis who loved those things that we all see, the birds and the flowers, the great garden, but who in the great garden also loved those things that we do not see, mischievous angels climbing trees, and above the trees, the spacious seats of paradise that await us with their invisible cushions of air, covered in flowers, which, says Saint Francis, will hold this body, *notre frère le corps,* upright when the trumpets will have sounded; Saint Francis loved this country in the spring and its blue voices, loved all these paintable things; and he'd had a special kindness for painters and for he whose pierced hand guided their hands across plaster, over walls; he who for a hundred years had been intervening on their behalf with the Almighty. Saint Francis wouldn't have given him a pig, he had more tact than that. He would have called him *frère Lorentino.* He would have said that name in the sacred French language that he loved, that he never spoke, but sang. He would have approached little Lorenzo at midday in summer; he wouldn't have had the face of some yokel, rather, those of fifty young monks in their blue frocks, or perhaps his very own face, unique, emaciated, and princely beneath tonsure, with Dame Poverty at one arm, beautiful as a lily, and at his other *sa petite sœur la Mort,* Dame Death, beautiful as a lily and whiter still, or perhaps out of modesty he would have come with the features of a wealthy commissioner, Sixtus, a Medici, or why not Sigismondo Pandolfo Malatesta returned from above in war harness with a handfull of gold, gold in his warrior's grasp that he'd always kindly reserved for painters. And in the words of Saint Francis, his French song, or in the silence if he had said nothing, Lorentino would have suddenly seen and understood perspective, seen the mathematical skeleton that

Trust This Sign

keeps bodies upright, understood anatomy, all thanks to the peeling back of the particular layers of body and soul, this obscure optical jumble out of which universals are born straight away, leaving this jumble behind, in the brightness of midday. Lorentino would have read all of this quite clearly; and with an understanding of the jumble, and a forgetting of that understanding, he too would have traced universal shapes into the plaster of San Francesco.

He looked at Diosa, Angioletta, Bartolomeo; he wanted to ask them why, how, but didn't. There was nothing more to it: one masters these shapes by looking; they have nothing to say. Saint Francis or some other had done that for Piero. And so why not for Lorentino?

The wind doesn't respond; Angioletta, her expression calm, her gestures calm, leaves the table and doesn't speak; the fire burns down, you can't hear it now so it feels as if the wind is picking up, is coming into the house, is within these masses of shadow in the corners; it's he. These shadowy caparisons in the countryside aren't olive trees; it's he. Were Sigismondo Pandolfo not in hell, it would be he, but; it's the wind. And *le Chemin de Saint Jacques* up above, the Milky Way, the standard of the world, the paused lightning bolt that travels the breadth of the sky, the long halo above what head—is it he? The farmer never looks so high; he recognizes his olive trees, his vines; the great horseman is hurrying him along; he speeds down the final slope and sees the little light in his house below, old Maria's light, against which the black army is bridling. Sigismondo's hounds, one black one white, stop. He finally pushes open the door, which swings open and clatters against the wall with all the wind, and this racket feels comforting to him. Old Maria sees that he no longer has the pig. He tells her his story and his ramblings aren't confused, they understand each other well; he says that his painter is a fatso, is a rascal; they laugh. "Good Saint Martin" says the old woman while laughing. In San Francesco, armor is stirring: the wind has finally managed to open a door and has slammed it open against a wall, little silver objects tumbling to the ground. They roll on the ground and stop, unseen; Constantine doesn't awaken, it seems that he is dreaming of angels, but it's only plaster; below, in Arezzo, Lorentino who once mixed this plaster looks at the littlest of his sons, who is puffing out his cheeks, exhaling into the pig's bladder. It sounds like a trumpet. Lorentino lies down and quickly falls to sleep.

During the night, Saint Martin came to him. The saint seemed angry; he was wearing a harness like that of Sigismondo Pandolfo but his face was that of the Ferrarese painter seen long ago in Sienna of whom Lorentino had been thinking only the day before. One hand was on the hilt of his sword, the other hand was holding his helmet, and his wrath seemed more formidable for its being contained within the poise of a horseman's coat that fell smoothly to his ankles, flaring out around a chivalric stance—a gray-haired warrior distinguished by many battles. The wind had stopped. Lorentino wasn't moving, was pretending to sleep; an animated light fell on his closed eyes. It didn't surprise him that the saint had grown old, as old as his former bishopric in Gaul; it didn't surprise him that the saint had come wearing the battle-dress of his youth. Martin remained silent for a moment, looking around irritably and moving his mouth without making a sound, like a man who has been insulted and who is deciding whether to reply with something even worse; but this anger was a maternal embrace, an embrace in which you could be a little boy with nothing to fear; you wanted to be with this fury, to be with her and to smolder with her in her great fire. Lorentino opened his eyes like a child who, sensing his mother at the foot of his bed, pretends he's asleep to keep her from leaving. He stared at the heavy, gathered brows. "God," said the saint, "has commissioned a painting from you. And you dare to haggle?" These words did not seem to mollify the holy one, but neither did they irritate him further: his holy anger burned pure as a star; it bore Lorentino no malice, it was as benevolent as the blue voices, although the saint spoke in the same tone as a captain who points out to his dull-witted horsemen both the hill to be taken as well as how to take it. Lorentino said nothing. And with that voice that had come to him across the layers of eternity, that each day spoke to God the Father but which nonetheless had the air of having just emerged from a grove where a captain was quartering his troops, the saint continued: "Those whom you call your masters, who do you think commissions them?" In a flash of lightning, Lorentino saw Piero. "And who has been yours these years and has never forgotten you despite your retard in executing his orders? They all knew the instant they first touched their brushes. But you, you think it's Sixtus, Sigismondo, Piero, or a farmer who wants a painting. What do you think they would do with such things?" Lorentino, who heard these words clearly, who wasn't afraid, thought about the look the old irascible Ferrarese had given him up in Sienna, who was now before him again but whose body then had housed the soul of an old gothic painter without a commission, not that of a saint: Lorentino had a better understanding of that look now. The saint had said what he had come to say, he was thinking about moving on, his anger was already burning elsewhere. Nonetheless he said: "Your painting is worth a pig, or the city of Rome, which is to say nothing." He turned around, his impeccable coat not stirring, the pieces of his war harness grating against themselves but making no sound; the horseman turned to leave, neither walking nor floating, his spurs glinting. Lorentino, lying on his back and propped up on his elbows to watch him leave, found all of this peculiar, but it moved him. The saint donned his helmet as he passed through the door. The wind began again, Martin was back on his horse. Sigismondo's hounds were at his heels, black and white, running through the countryside. Again Lorentino saw Piero in the dark, but he had never seen him this way before, as if Piero were his brother. As if he were going into San Francesco with Piero, as if they were passing through the door the wind had opened and lifting their candles high above them in the Bacci chapel so filled with paintings, as if together they were looking: he saw the little sign an emperor received in a dream, this little object not even so much an object, but which was held at arm's length as one holds a candle and which manages to fluster both flanks of Maxence's minions, all the sundered battlery, a thousand Moorish warriors to the left, a thousand Gaulish horsemen on the right. He wanted to see this sign in Piero's eyes as well, but Piero had disappeared, Lorentino was all alone. The great patron was before him.

Trust This Sign

THE NEXT DAY, LORENZO began the Saint Martin, which he would complete within the time upon which he and the farmer had agreed. And he did it in the old style or the new, the gothic manner or the antique, which seemed somehow fresher, with the soft Siennese touch or the Florentine precision, all those things that don't matter; and he made it with anger and charity, which matter, anger lived becoming charity painted, dedicating himself to it and refining it layer upon layer, devotionally; and, what also matters, he made it with forms that you see in space, upon which charity does its work, and amongst them men, trees, hats. We don't know whose features he gave to the saint and whose to the beggar. But it was what we call a masterpiece, so to speak, of a minor master or a master. Perhaps it was the most beautiful thing made of color and line that man had ever brought to bear on the face of the Earth; it was along the same road as Piero, but going to the end of that road and passing him by; it was to Piero what Piero was to Veneziano, what midday is to morning. And in this case it took place in a town piazza, and with a noble sword and a fine body that stood straight up, each and both radiating a solidity, a soulfulness as the coat was cleaved in two, with great solemnity, a sullen saint and a sullen beggar, a sullen horse, and all three infinitely happy to be standing there sullenly; a reasonable brightness fell on the porticoes and in the foreground, a young woman passing by looked at something on the ground but didn't lower her head, haughty, dreamy, sullen, we do not see what she was looking at, he hadn't painted the bunch of grapes, her hands were open like a Madonna of mercy; and on her head, an Oriental miter. It was Lorentino's life plain and simple, as if by Piero, but by Lorentino.

And of course Saint Martin wasn't capable of such a miracle, only the Son made flesh would have known how to do such a thing, and not even he; it was too late in Lorentino's life for such an inconceivable object to burst from his old hand, his anger was too dulled for so much charity to be released. So this was more in the delicious manner of a minor Marches colorist, a good storyteller, and in this great Dalmatian garden he was painting, Lorentino said then and there his master Piero's lessons, which is to say use only perspective, the antique; but freely, playing and laughing under the yoke, like hunting dogs responding to their master's horn, but nonetheless rejoicing at the hunt itself. And in the middle of this sky filling with intoxication and song, Lorentino made the little piece of the beyond, the halo that was his hallmark, that he fleur-de-lysed and contoured in all that gold; and so set forth, the saint cut the coat in two with the hands of a seamstress, smooth and elated, fussy, he hadn't gotten off his horse, was leaning like a young mother toward the beggar; and as a last touch, a serious child holding the bridle and looking out at you, a child who was Hope made flesh, an angel or a little valet, his cheeks red, his bare feet amongst the violets of the woods. Lorentino enjoyed adding them. Who can know what it looked like. But it was a masterpiece, since Lorentino had given the best he had to give, had devoted himself as one should, just as each of us, doing the best we can, devoting ourselves as best we can, doubtless makes a masterpiece.

Diosa watched him carefully the whole time he worked on the painting: because all the while he had the touch she had long ago felt, but she didn't know what he was using it on now. She told herself that perhaps she would have some dresses, or maybe Angioletta would, now.

And Bartolomeo had his master. The disciple watched a master at work, between Ash Wednesday and Easter. We don't know what he did with this, perhaps a masterpiece of his own as he approached his sixtieth year, perhaps nothing.

THE FARMER RETURNED on the agreed date and found the painting very pretty but didn't make a big deal about it, out of fear that the painter would ask for more. But he didn't. The farmer had brought his cart and put it on the back, because it was big. It was nearing Easter in the countryside. The village curate also found it pretty, in the secluded village of Saint-Martin's church, where of course this saint should be. The curate added a gilded wooden cornice. Old Maria also saw it, impressed either by the illusion of space or by the gold, but she didn't quite recognize her Saint Martin; other farmers saw it, and beneath it took off their bonnets and pondered, but no lords and no captains saw it, they didn't come through very often. Lorentino died. No trumpets were heard. The farmer died; old Maria had long since joined her Saint Martin, whose face no one knew. And the Ferrarese who looked like a Masaccio or a Saint Martin had fallen as well, all alone with his cane in the rough-hewn countryside, between two commissions he'd been denied. And no trumpets were heard. Occasionally at night the wind from the Verna, the same wind, banged into the wall of this little church the way it had down below on the churches of Arezzo. Sigismondo's dogs, one black, one white, were yapping at the doors. Occasionally, they would open a door. And at midday in summer on the little piazza before this church and on the piazza before San Francesco there was no one, only long shadows and light for no one. Vasari stopped there fifty years later, he went into this country church, he didn't see the Lorentino, they had put up something newer that Vasari didn't like very much; the Lorentino was in the sacristy, resting peacefully with a chasuble hung from one of its corners; Vasari didn't go in, he didn't write a *Life of Lorentino.* Perhaps it was the most beautiful thing made of color and line that man had ever made on the face of the Earth. This work unknown by Vasari remained in the sacristy for a long time. Vasari died. During the French wars, or those of the Hapsburgs, the parish became very poor; there was a big hole in the wall of the sacristy, perhaps from a cannonball, or perhaps only from time: and as they didn't have any money, they put the painting there to cover the hole, so that in the peace before a mass the curate could dress in private, praying for Saint Martin's help and not suffering from the Vernal winds. This for ten years; fifty. And as the back of the wood of this painted surface was cooking ceaselessly, was taking in water and freezing, the image began to warp and became horrible, or laughable; "Good Saint Martin" said the farmers, laughing, when they saw it; they turned the painting over, out of decency. Saint Martin impassive, abruptly Florentine or softly Siennese, disfigured but impassive, watched the wind off the Verna, the long shadows and no one. It was not the most beautiful thing there is to see on this earth. The heavens afflict those things they love. Skies golden and rose were changing. Saint Martin was becoming soot, colors were falling; one would have been able to see Lorentino's underdrawings, the first features added the first morning when he was still filled with his vision of the saint, the theological hand and its beginnings, its furies. One would have been able to see it all. But no one passed by there, it overlooked fallow fields. Along the bank, nettles grew, and violets; lost pigs and sparrows passed. At night, signs blazed, a forest in flames, comets. One night the saint didn't see the signs, he no longer had a face: there was nothing more to see, the parish got back on its feet, the wall was rebuilt and this nothing was tossed away. Today it is dust, like Lorentino; like Piero; like the name Lorentino; like the name of Saint Martin that farmers no longer call, that no longer bursts forth in their laughter and no longer cries along with them, that is held silent in mouths below ground. Here and there the name Piero is spoken, is multiplied and divided into nothingness. It won't be long now. One day, God will no longer hear one name before any other. He will send a sign to the seven. They will raise seven trumpets to their lips.

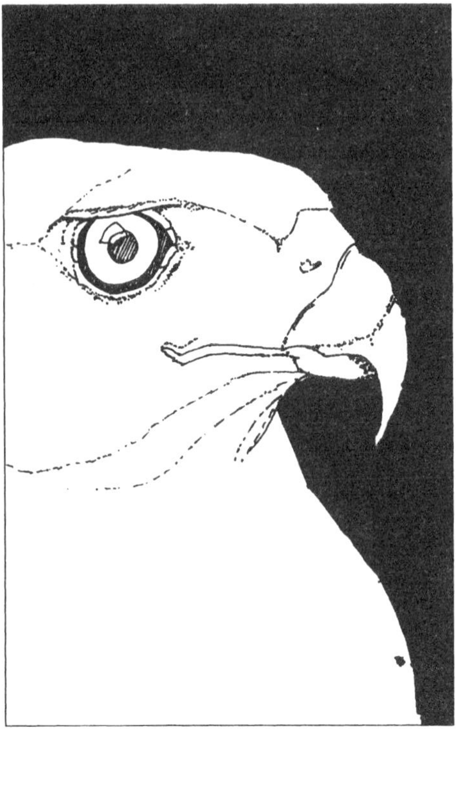

The King of the Wood

for Gérard Macé

> Their faces breathed anger;
> forgoing words, they growled;
> they frequented the forests like
> sitting rooms.
>
> OVID, *Metamorphoses*

I, GIAN DOMENICO DESIDERII, I worked for twenty years with that old fool. They tell me he still hasn't decided whether or not to die; from time to time I'll hear bits of news, praise blown his way; sometimes I'll see another recent product with the same trees, the same sheepfolds, the same palaces at sunrise, and that same sky up above, like a pit. Doubtless the same splendors, the same marvels. I've had my fill but he's kept his appetite, the fat little fool, the good apostle. And if it makes him happy, he should still paint. And stew in his great devotion. I was a painter, once, and now I'm a prince. Almost a prince: I reign over thieves and deaf-mutes, carriages and liveries, coaches; and I reign over forests; in this low world I am constable and pissboy, factotum to the Monseigneur de Nevers, Duke Charles, who holds Mantua.

It rains in Mantua. It is a sad town, the sort that always seems muddy even when the sun is out. This muddiness is my business. Where have they gone, the great expectations that drove one to paint with sun in one's face and in one's soul, surrounded by the scent of the pines? Where have you gone, little men made by my hand, obedient gods, knaves lost in floppy felt hats and sailors lost in dreams, passersby fording streams? But they must be there, I call them in through the rain to the sheepfolds, they smell of drink and wet dogs, these knaves of mine, my thieves. Their floppy hats are dripping into their eyes, I can barely see their faces; it's as though they are being eaten away, as though they are being swallowed by their beards, or by the rain, the anguish of morning that sends the wolves home. Is that Jean or Giovanni? I'm fairly certain that's Hakem; he's as black as soot. Come boys, on your horses. Once again through the forest, sounding our horns and waving madly, and tonight, deep within us, exhausted at last, our souls are at rest. Open your eyes wide, knaves: deep in this mad mix are all the little beasts you never see but to kill; they pay you to find and kill them, and with what you earn you get blind drunk and sleep a little easier. Look at the shadows around us. How they carry us off. They say it is morning. It is summer. We are galloping, that much is sure. I can't even see the floppy hats now, in all this falling I can't even hear the hoofbeats. Are branches cracking above us? We don't hear them either. Wild boars are charging, or perhaps only tree stumps: which will move, which will stay still? And this unarmed prey, steeped from tip to toe in uncertainty, in impotence—you, old trees, are you succumbing too?

I PAINTED TO BE A PRINCE.

I was about twelve. It was the middle of summer, at that hour of the evening when it is hot still, but the shadows are shifting. I was running pigs back to trough, through an oak forest near Nemi, below a big road; I was nibbling a loaf and having a high time smacking the fat, clumsy beasts that moved under my hand. But I was growing tired of them and turned my attention to beheading the ferns and haughty flowers of the undergrowth, my violence filling the air with perfume; my little flail kept me busy and content. From far off, I heard a heavy coach advancing slowly; I hid and kept still: the summer sun was beating down on the road and I was there in the shadows, invisible, no higher than the ground itself, watching this sunny road. In the summer light, ten feet from me and my pigs, a coach stopped, painted and emblazoned with bands of blue; a girl in all her finery burst out of the emblazoned box, laughing, running, as if toward me; I could see her white teeth, her bright eyes; still laughing, she stopped at the edge of the shadows, resolutely turned her back on me, stood for an interminable instant in the sunlight, marbled by the shadows of leaves—her hair, her enormous azure skirts, the white of her hands and the gold of her cuffs, all of it blazing—and when in a dream those hands went to her skirts and lifted them, her prodigious thighs and ass were given to me like daylight, but darkly; brutally, she crouched and pissed. I was trembling. The golden flow fell somberly in the sunlight, making a hole in the moss. The girl was no longer laughing, was now preoccupied with keeping her skirts up out of the way and with feeling this rude light leaving her; her head was cocked slightly, inert, she pondered the hole she was making in the grass. Her azure frock was puffed up around her neck, crackling, inflated, extravagantly displaying her loins. The painted door of the carriage was slightly ajar, the pisseuse having only lightly pushed it shut, and behind it a man was looking out the window, wearing a ruffled silk doublet, watching her. He had as much lace around his neck as she had around her ass; he was smiling the way people smile when they think no one is watching, with a mix of disdain and pleasure, both modest and smug, and with a ferocious tenderness. The coachman was looking away, civilized and beastly. The rush from the beauty ran dry; the prince made some pleasantry, and then said a word reserved for the lowliest tarts; he smiled more openly, more tenderly. The woman's hands tightened around the lace she was clutching, and she made a nervous little laugh, perhaps servile, perhaps beseeching or overjoyed, which excited me; she had lifted her head, and she too was looking at him. I imagined this look as blood. High white flowers bloomed by my cheek. An indifferent violence rose around me like the midday sky, like the tops of the trees.

In one bound the woman was standing, the ordinary blaze of her skirts replacing the very different blaze of her thighs; she returned to the carriage, more slowly than before, with a complaisance and affectation to her steps; she was blushing; she lowered her eyes, she was not smiling. The prince, yes. She sat before him with a rustling of silks. He lowered his hand, grabbed a fistful of her skirts, then, ceremonious, remote, tapped two fingers on the outside of the door: the horses and the coachman, but parts of the carriage, obeyed this little noise they knew so well, and docilely steered their delicate cargo for Rome, a cargo made of a substance different from the wood of carriages and the leather of harnesses, made from different flesh from that of coachmen and horses, a flesh that nevertheless, like that of horses, pisses and stares, but which has the time and the inclination to make fun of one or the other, to piss more bestially than a horse and to make fun of it, to stare more intensely than a coachman does at his road in the dead of night and to make fun of it, a flesh that wears lace about its loins as if in promise of some sweeter flesh, or which wears it around a collar to distinguish it from flesh, to reduce it to name alone, éclat, disdain, this finer flesh of princes. So this jumble of flesh moved off, dust rising from the road as though behind a flock of sheep.

I don't know if what I experienced that day may be called pleasure, I was still little. I visited the spot where she had lifted her skirts; I went to the spot where the carriage had stopped, the little consecrated place where I calculated that the prince had been; I looked at the edge of the woods, the exact tree underneath which the girl had pissed for her prince. I lowered what I could imagine of a white hand, I said aloud the word used for the lowest whores; I tapped my two fingers. In this light the trees were immense, numerous, tireless. So we are made that here, in this light, flesh takes on a greater weight. God, who sees everything with an even eye—we do not envy such even sight; we envy the sight of those who pause patiently to consider what they will soon devour, while all around them the world explodes. Sitting there on that road in the bright sunshine, where a prince who perhaps had been only a marquis had, for a moment, smiled, I began to cry, loudly, in great sobs. I would rather have burned. An insane elation took hold of me that perhaps was pain, anger, or the disturbed laughter of those who suddenly find God along a road. It was the future, without question, this bucket of tears. Just as easily, it was God, in his curious fashion.

I had observed the nudity of many other women. I also knew the improvident use they made of it, moving beneath men, so deeply present but with all their strength withdrawn, fighting with this nothing that fulfills them. But as beautiful as they sometimes were, the ones I had seen busy at such enterprise had neither the white legs nor the great braids, and the dresses beneath which the cowhands had their fun were made of the shoddy stuff in which the better-born wrap what they eat and discard, but not right away, and not quite the same way, our grain or our women, our three ecus, our dead, our cheese. Above all, these women had seemed ashamed, and they hadn't known what to do about it, perhaps because they believed their shame concealed nothing; and how would they have been able to marvel at and abandon themselves to the clandestine filth that fills us and out of which perhaps we're made, they for whom filth was the norm, was like a second skin, like the air they breathed in the flocks and the decaying earth that spurted onto the nettles in the cowsheds, and the smell of sheep that was a permanent part of their low, laboring bodies that always toil, disconnected, screaming, always seem to be at work; and so always reek. To piss somberly, you need clean hands. Yes, this was some other flesh, another species altogether. And that species had appeared before me, evidently; I had had my Visitation; a celestial maiden of lace and azure had descended from one of those carriages out of some grand parade, had walked gracefully toward me under the trees on the satin of her little shoes, in all her finery had hitched up her skirts, trembling with the knowledge that she was profaning herself, had lightly splashed the satin of those little shoes. I would have given my life to see that again, but this time not while hiding beneath the trees. No, from the other side. Not as a coachman at his wit's end, inert, forced to look where his desires were not, and to see it all out of the corner of his eye for an instant all the same, seeing all that he won't have. No, from the other side completely, as daylight sees the earth, gives it rain or drought as it wills. I wanted to be the one who got to see this miracle every day, at every hour of the day, just for the tapping of two fingers; I wanted to be the one at whom the sacrosanct in all her profaned pomp would look, he whom she would await; that somber man who, with a lump in his throat, dares to smile, to make some remark, to decorate a crouching beauty with scathing little names meant for tarts. I called that a prince, in my high youth.

MY PARENTS WERE POOR DEVILS, without means and doubtless without wisdom, for which they didn't have the time. I think I loved them. They rented out their arms and mine, those of my brothers, to the fat farmers throughout the *Castelli,* farmers who themselves had only the barest grain in reserve, a bit of pork on the table, and on their straw mattresses, if they wanted them, young, heavyset girls smelling of sheep, with neither azure around their necks nor lace about their thighs: they were poor devils, they too. Me, I looked after pigs and sheep, sheep that are even dumber than pigs, and cows that are pitiful, inanimate. And so from flock to flock I was rented, the next season to Tivoli, on the grassy slopes presided over by palaces, palaces put there to justify and sustain such reigns with heaps of meat, leather, mounts: to such ends, shacks line the slopes, shacks in which beasts are left to guard other beasts. I was one of them. I didn't go into the palace, but I grazed my flocks the length of the roads that rise to meet them; many carriages passed by in which I could see monsignori in red and lace, captains with polished blades and lace, gentlemen with soft gloves, soft boots, soft silk doublets and lace, all with one Visitation or another facing them, these azure bawds, like the clumsy coachmen outside had horses before them. These emblazoned boxes passed through the villa roundabouts, slowly, like a mass, awkwardly, like hay wagons, brutally, like whips, climbing up the steep sandy slopes finer than flour, and the din of the wheels and the whips disappeared into the more massive din of waters falling from the muzzles of lions, the nostrils of cattle, the urns of old bearded gods and women leaning unfatigued, the fountains with a thousand faces that all these powerful men are crazy about. And I saw, flight after flight on the stairs high above, dresses twirling across the terraces, stirring slightly with breeze, entering the high buildings in which they are kept; a monsignore lagged a bit behind, was hanging back beneath the tall trees, all in red and as powerful as the trees, as visible, dreaming or perhaps praying, because God is as tall as the trees, because the trees make one raise an eye to God— and eventually he put a foot to the last step, more slowly, all in scarlet, entering the henhouse where one pecks at these azure birds, plucks them, eats them.

For the rest of the afternoon there was nothing else, the tall trees indefatigably rustled through the emptiness of the world, the splattering fountains flowed on as if unseen by passing armies, seasons. Cows were dreaming in the shade, I had made a little whistle out of bark into which I blew a single note till nightfall. Up above, little changed as the evening cooled, the doves that had been plucked had like phoenixes been reborn, redressing for a little meal, the tireless monsignori still hungry. We stared up at the long tables of people attended by a thousand footmen under the elms. I took my pigs to trough.

THERE WERE ALSO HORSEMEN.

Not the sort of horsemen who parade alongside coaches to stir the sweet hearts of women within, these young prelates or marquises, all the king's men: they remained on the road, only leaping into the fields to grab a gallop that would make certain hearts beat faster and my uncertain beasts run away, quickly returning to the road, trotting their horses close to the doors and chatting up those behind them; they only dismounted when they arrived up above, to the thunderous, hydraulic accompaniment of a fugue of fountains. The horsemen I mean were more reserved, they too liked to play around but they did so without pretense, since they weren't trying to land azure prey; there were no women with them, they were more enigmatic. They weren't boors but, out of bravado, they had taken on all the trappings of boors, their horses and their soft boots, though their boots weren't as soft as those of all the king's men, and, tacked on to this style borrowed from boors, they added the smiles of king's men, borrowed as well. This shocked me. They would go into the palaces, and the lackeys they passed would have their indifferent air, bestial, that they would affect when princes passed. And almost every day a few of them would ride into my meadows, putting their feet to the ground; they'd make some pleasantry, and I would run off to crouch a little farther afield, and there I'd pester them with my whistle. I'd spy on them between the leaves. Unhurried, they would settle in, lifting their heads, breathing the air, taking in the horizon with a neutral glance, the footpaths retreating through the fields, the herds; they might exchange a few words, hesitating or disagreeing, and then they'd make some sudden, grand gesture toward something that seemed to be wildly interesting to them down there, toward a meagre stand with a little waterfall, at the edge of a wood where day and night seemed to be fighting over the foliage like they do all summer long, a struggle yielding nothing more than leaves: so they pointed at various things, each showing the others, and even I looked, opening my eyes wide to better see what was so shocking down there, perhaps a beautiful woman sleeping in those woods, or why not pissing, or a real Visitation rising into the sky, but there was nothing but leaves and water, sky. I blew my whistle. Their ludicrous ecstasy soon abated, and from their holsters they took little things, their papers and leads, and settled in, standing tall in their boots or sitting on an embankment, endlessly making little drawings. But of course—these were the painters.

The painters. But not all of them, that is to say not all of them together at the same time, in the same place, because there were certain affinities, camps with daggers drawn against others or devouring each other like wasps in a jar; old Cavalier d'Arpin and Pietro Testa, Sacchi and Pietro Berrettini de Cortone, Valentin de Boulogne, Gérard de la Nuit, Poussin, Mochi, Swanevelt and the two Claudes, Claude Mellan, and Claude Lorrain; occasionally, you even saw that drunken clown with them, Pieter van Laer, known as *il Bamboccio*, gimpy and misbegotten, with coarser boots but without the boorish airs, since he wasn't really one of them; but never *il Cavaliere* Bernini, who was the biggest fish in this ocean and had far better things to do with his time. It was a Congregation of Virtuosi, *les Académiciens de Saint Luc*, dowered by Barberini far more than by Saint Luc, so they were Barberini's band; these Barberinis whom one never saw there because they were forever psalming at Saint Peter's; both Barberinis, Maffeo with his tiara and the little braids, and Taddeo who had the more substantial braids, the purse strings; these two and a hundred others, all of the interminable king's men, Francesco and the two Antonios, all the little Italian names, all of whom wore fiery moiré, braided hats, miters, robes, and lambskins, and all of whom had three bees in their coats of arms and who used such titles to buzz through Saint Peter's, or through Castel Gandolfo or the Latran, in the leafy villas of Tivoli, in Frascati, even buzzing up to the smallest hill where there was surely just enough water for it to come crashing back down into basins, watching water collapse with blank stares, making honey in the mellifluous coffers of the palace, the gardens, the churches—all these men with bees in their tabards hired the painters. For in order to build and decorate such coffers, churches, or palaces, in order to make the wax into which Maffeo and Taddeo, the two Antonios, the whole swarm, could consume their meats, their women, all the books written in all the languages since Saint Peter, and, in return could spew out gold, writs that kill, that pardon, that absolve those they kill, could spew out the balloons bursting across Europe, the Latin that beckons angels, and the church songs that swing wide the doors to mortal souls—it takes a lot of painters to cover these Godly hives in honey, painters who then labored in this honey, struggling to see the world or pretending to, while from this commerce also gleaning a little honey for themselves, in passing. And to manage this, these painters weren't willing just to consume things, to devour books, meats, women; they actually had to apply themselves, had to crouch down and do some gilding, had to demean themselves, to work, to practice their craft. So that's the reason for their little bazaar in Tivoli, collecting their pollen in my pastures, mimicking the princes while peering at the horizon from on high, but returning home to paint like boors, up to their elbows in gold just as I had blood and gore up to mine when my ewes gave birth, when I delivered them. But who will deliver them?

The King of the Wood

I know all of this now, but that cowherd, the little swineherd, he didn't know a thing. I didn't know their names, I didn't even know that Barberini was their patron saint. The swineherd watched men with big hats and beards do delicate little work, like women darning socks.

I grew used to their little routines, but I remained apart from them. Soon, if they hadn't shown up for several days, I'd get impatient for their arrival—they often preferred the other side, the Cascatelles, beautiful, useless rocks where nothing grows. I waited for them, invoked them by various magics: I pretended to be one of them, I gestured expansively toward some point on the horizon and tried to concentrate on it at length, my head cocked to the side, very serious and very stupid, but nothing came of it. And when they would finally return, I'd be upset that they were there. I was a lost child, whom nothing and no one could amuse. I didn't know where I would find amusement. And then they'd be there and I'd move my flock a little, all of us fiddling off on our own, not making a show of noticing each other, I with my whistles and three jay-feathers, some bits of wicker, and they with their papers and their leads; the blue of my jay feathers seemed sadder, smaller. But all of this was in the order of things, undoubtedly; one day, that order will fall.

VERY EARLY ONE MORNING, I went to cut whistles down below a thicket, along one of those humid banks from which trembling scents rise, stirred by the lightest breeze; a bank of willows and aspens beneath which the low species gather, grass snakes, frogs: the best whistles come from the bark of these trees, whistles from which one can draw long fat moans, like those of frogs. And yes, God knows I didn't go there just to look for good whistles. The odor of rotting leaves mounted, and leaning into it I advanced cautiously, preoccupied, my eyes fixed on the ground. The June dawn found me through this low wood. By a detour through a breach in the trees, I saw far before me high on a hill the facade of a palace in the rising sun: nothing moved there, no one stirred, it was as bright and uninhabited as a rock; here, in the wood, the nighttime mists persisted, the foliage was unfolding, all was black. I felt good. I began to sing a song of my own invention that I was secretly nourishing, that I often returned to and embellished to my liking in the gimpy language that then was my domain; it had something to do with my azure pisseuse; with certain other riches; and with a Visitation whose great generosity tosses such riches into the heart of a swineherd. I rejoiced at this prayer, and in my excitement I stripped many more branches than I needed: I sang at the top of my lungs; I pranced around; the palace up above was blazing as though it were my song; it was calling to me, I flew toward it, I held it in my hand, slept on it and clutched it; the three notes of the hoopoe were my response, golden and distant as a sleeping palace. Tears came to my eyes: my mother cried the same way, the poor woman, when, bowed, the Visitation, Our Lady in Procession, passed above her. The sky shimmered: day had broken, it sneaked in beneath the willows, and in this half-light a white mask was smiling. My tears froze on my cheeks. The hoopoe's cry drew nearer. The mask was blackly mustached, with thick lips and strong teeth that gleamed in a smile; there was another white something in the shadows, some paper that the mask was holding. This sheet and this mask paused, breathing, making two large bright spots of the same size, the double ocelli of a very big, black butterfly, its invisible wings trembling in the willows; I was beneath this trembling. I don't know if I was afraid, it seemed benevolent; it wasn't a flying thing: just a very dark, stocky man whom I had already seen. The large, pale face and the jet black hair belonged to Claude Lorrain.

Something bolted beneath the leaves; I turned on my heels and ran. I hadn't even left my hiding place when a hand grabbed me behind the collar and lifted me off the ground. I didn't struggle, I had seen him enough to know that the big black butterfly was a giant. He put me down, turned me toward him without letting me go, and spoke to me sweetly the way you talk to a scared animal. I wasn't listening: the sun now shone in the tall trees, their leaves trembling with this bright bounty as they do in the worst of storms, in the deadest calms, at midday as at dawn, everywhere at last awaking, the palace shutters rattling, opening under someone's hands, and in my wooden head as in the rustling skies pealing bells resonated, rose, giving peace to nothing, the fury of the pounding bells making everything seem forgotten, disappeared, the final words of the prayer to the Visitation that, like my life, I had gotten from my mother, like my fear, like my shame: *now and at the hour of our death.* I repeated this from my depths like a bird singing the same three notes over and over. Perhaps I too said them aloud. All that time Claude held me, and I felt his breath on my face. I felt a little better, and I saw up close this sort of turnip he had for a face; I understood perhaps that in looking at me he remembered something long past, or was trying to. The color returned to my cheeks, he smiled. Still looking into my eyes he began to hum, and soon was singing at length, in its entirety, in a lovely voice, the exact words of my song, the carriage and the blue dress, the golden flow. No one but I had ever sung these words. He held in his laughter as he was singing, and when he came to the silly refrain in which I was praying to the queen of Heaven for a pisseuse of my own, he laughed with his mouth wide open. He held my collar tighter and said that the riches of my song would be mine, however little good they'd do me. With an open hand he made a broad gesture to the visible horizon, the sun, the trees, and the palace, as if he were also showing all that one couldn't see in the palace, the doves, the Madonnas: "All of this," he said, "is yours, if you enter into my service." He had relaxed his grip, I was free; I fell where he dropped me, I cried every tear in my little body. Seated, he waited without looking at me. I think that the hoopoe let out its three notes once more, three little sacks of honey in the woods. I remained and followed him.

ARE THESE FALCONS YOU'RE loosing, my sweets? Just so. They are our hunters when we can no longer see. It won't be honey they'll sew into the loins of rabbits, of hoopoes—O enough little songs! Birds both beautiful and large that sing to mate and that stink, they too, the unfortunates. You understand these hoopoes, don't you, Hakem? No one eats them, but… You're not talking. Hard at it, then, my sweets! You see nothing, but you don't need eyes to kill: our falcons see for us, are our eyes and our beaks that by some marvel flow away from us when we remove their cowls. They return full of blood, with feathers barely still. Quails? Something else? Come, the duke will be content, he will have hazel grouse on his table tonight. And I will have his wife. I will dry my gear, have a drink, another, will go tranquilly to her room and plunge into his bowl of milk. How everything is simple and dark beyond this milk.

There is nothing in the woods. You know well, my little

partridges, nothing but meat. Perhaps that is why at night you swim deep into your wine casks to drown. Not the best of lives but, after all, it makes good hunters, right? What comes over you, now and again, on beautiful days? Your heads tilt back, you fall still, a hare slips your grip, a hatchet dangles from your fingertips, a musket falls, and your horse senses that he too can relax, can breathe the air, your weight on him has changed, no longer are you this tensed pile of meat that has always terrified him, whose dark black weight he's been lugging around, no, the darkness has departed and you are light, you look at the magic dust that the sun sprinkles into the glade, you stop in its midst and remain there, it warms you, and not only your body—what has come over you? Are you listening to that cavalry on high? Is it hunting your little soul, carrying it off, tending it gently? You lift your head higher, it's all too blue, you can't see anything anyway; but even the ferns seem greener—and your faces, my princes, are they the same? It's only wind. It leaves quickly, you are gone with your mount, all the weight of darkness drills a huge hole in the brush, and in that hole there are only branches that crack, trembling little bones that escape the falcon but crack between the teeth of the fox, and, if the whole world were in your fist, it too would crack just the same. My sweets.

But no magic dust today: only more of this soupy fog that so easily leads to ire, and to those detestable things that storm around us and that we desire. The drops never tire of beating the earth. Curse the world, it will reward you.

Notes

The ambition of these few mentions is minor: to catalogue a handful of items sure to elude a good American dictionary or encyclopedia. Noted are a few French phrases and historical references, and one countermeasure is taken against a potential catastrophe of mistaken identity.

THE LIFE OF JOSEPH ROULIN

Henri Riviere. 1827–1883; French Naval officer, defended Hanoi in 1882.

Le casseur des assiettes. Literally, the plate-breaker; a vendor of china and flatware in a traditional open market who would bark out a sales pitch: "A lovely service for eight! Sixty-four pieces! Just fifteen francs! Buy 'em, or I start breaking 'em!"

Le temps des cerises. Cherry-picking time, a line from a popular song of the period about spring.

Sur le motif. An artists' term, used to describe the painting of landscapes, or the act of placing an easel in no particular spot and proceeding to paint whatever lies in the distance.

Le Grand Soir, or "Great Eve." An expression coined by the idealistic members of the post-revolutionary republican proletariat, denoting the eve of the installation of the "true" republic.

As *le Grand Soir* is the eve, *la Sociale* is the day.

Antoine Quentin Fouquier-Tinville. 1746–1795; political official, magistrate; condemned men to death by guillotine during the period known as "The Terror."

Baron Jean Baptiste Anacharsis de Cloots. 1755–1794; founder of anti-clergy movement, "The cult of reason"; guillotined.

GOD IS NEVER THROUGH

The Pardo. As distinct from The Prado. El Pardo Palace is located a few miles outside of Madrid and was built in the sixteenth century by Charles I. The paintings of the King's Antechamber described in the story were moved many years later to the Prado Museum, located on the Paseo del Prado, in Madrid. The Prado Museum was built in 1820 and was first devoted to Spain's natural history collections, not to its art.

The Prado mentioned in the story is therefore the boulevard, not the museum. The Pardo, the palace. *Viator emptor!*

PIERRE MICHON was born in Creuse, France, in 1945. His first work of fiction was published in 1984, and since that time his reputation as one of the foremost contemporary French writers has become well established. He has won many prizes, including the Prix France Culture for his first book, *Small Lives;* the Prix Louis Guilloux for the French edition of *The Origin of the World;* and the Prix de la Ville de Paris in 1996 for his body of work. He has also received the Grand Prix du Roman de l'Académie française for his novel *The Eleven,* the Grand Prix Société des gens de lettres de France (SGDL) for Lifetime Achievement in 2004, and the Prix Décembre (2002) and Petrarca-Preis (2010).

WYATT MASON, a contributing writer for the *New York Times Magazine* and a contributing editor at *Harper's,* has translated writing by Pierre Michon, Éric Chevillard, Michel de Montaigne, and Arthur Rimbaud. He teaches at Bard College.